Maritime Mysteries

and the Ghosts Who Surround Us

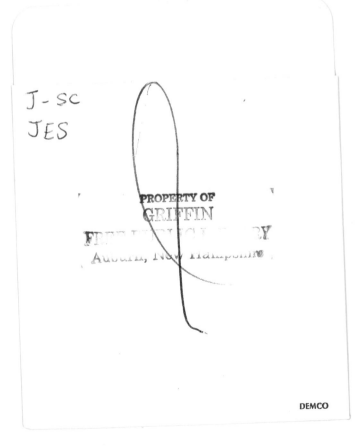

Dedicated with love to my grandchildren,
Michelle, Glenna, Glenn, and Jonathon,
and in memory of my wife, Rose.

Maritime Mysteries
and the Ghosts Who Surround Us

Bill Jessome

NIMBUS
PUBLISHING

Nimbus Publishing Limited
PO Box 9301, Station A
Halifax, NS B3K 5N5
(902) 455-4286

Design: Margaret Issenman, MGDC

Printed and bound in Canada

Canadian Cataloguing in Publication Data
Jessome, Bill
Maritime mysteries
ISBN 1-55109-291-3
1. Ghost stories, Canadian (English)—Maritime Provinces.   2. Tales—Maritime Provinces.
I. Title

GR113.5.M37J47 1999   398.2'09715'05   C99-950141-0

Nimbus Publishing acknowledges the financial support of the Canada Council and the Department of Canadian Heritage.

Table of Contents

We know what we are, but know not what we may be.
William Shakespeare

Foreword

It didn't go well the first time Uncle Bill and I faced a TV camera together. It was in the early 1960s and I was one of many children invited to the CJCB Television staff Christmas party that year. As the party neared its end someone on the crew decided it would look good for Bill to open that evening's newscast with one of the children on his knee. He picked me. Now, I am certain Bill had no idea back then that I would follow him into television news. No, I suspect it was Bill's keen sense of style and image that had him choose the child whose clothes best complimented his suit.

My memory of those first moments on a TV newscast has me squirming and crying and being quickly rescued by my mother. Uncle Bill's sudden serious tone and "TV Newsguy" delivery startled me. But that's not how Bill tells the story. My first chance to hear him recount the incident came thirty years later when we were hosting a segment of the Christmas Daddies Children's Telethon in that same Sydney studio. Fortunately, he told the story when we were not on air. According to Uncle Bill, it wasn't tears that spoiled my first TV appearance. Rather, a liquid of another sort ruined his suit. And I wasn't rescued by my mother; I was tossed to her and Uncle Bill was left reading the news damp and disgusted.

Actually, I don't think this version is true. But to watch and hear Bill tell it you can't help but believe the story. His delivery, his flair for detail, that conspiratorial glint in his eyes as he shares something secret with you. Heck, I want to believe the tale even when the laughs are at my expense.

Bill's love of story grew in his decades-long career as a television newscaster and reporter. That love brought him to his second career, that he began after his "retirement" at age sixty-five. Bill Jessome's *Maritime Mysteries* series ranks among the most successful segments of ATV's popular *Live at Five* news show. He and his favourite cameraman, the late Kevin MacDonald, brought every story to life in a way that created a strong demand for more.

Uncle Bill's decision to launch a new career as "man of mystery" did not surprise those of us fortunate enough to know him, not just his TV personality. His passion in life, second only to his love for his late wife Rose, is the telling of a good tale. I've watched him work out many of these stories over his favourite Sunday dinner. He would wink and smile and play with his inflection until he had the reaction he wanted from a captive audience.

Now, at age seventy-four, Bill has found a new way to share his stories. You are holding it in your hand. As you read some of his favourites you can almost hear that warm, familiar rasp in his voice—the sound that somehow made the stories more frightening. As for the likelihood of some of these tales, it really doesn't matter. Bill makes you want to believe them, just as he makes me want to believe I ruined his suit so many years ago.

—Phonse Jessome

Introduction

Questions and rarely a definitive answer: "Do you believe in ghosts, Mr. Jessome?"

"No, but I'm afraid of them." Certainly not very original, I admit, but it does break the ice when the conversation turns to the paranormal.

Like many people, I sometimes feel compelled to look over my shoulder. And for no particular reason occasionally, when I'm alone in my car at night driving down a lonely stretch of road, a foreboding sweeps over me. It's as if there were an invisible passenger seated beside me. I also fight the urge to glance in the rear-view mirror, afraid of what may be staring back.

Questions and more questions: "Explain, please, the puff of cold air that sweeps over my face when all the doors and windows are tightly closed. And explain away, if you can, the sickening odour of decaying flowers that wake me from a troubled sleep. And what is that standing at the foot of my bed?" I don't know. But I've been there.

And still more questions. "How old is the ghost story?"

"Older than me and thee, my inquisitive friend. The ghost story predates literature. It belongs to a primordial world; perhaps even during its blackness."

A word was brought to me in secret, and my ears heard a whisper of it.
It was during a nightmare when people are in deep sleep.
I was trembling with fear; all my bones were shaking.
A spirit glided past my face, and all the hair on my body stood on it,
The spirit stopped, but I could not see what it was...

From the book of Job. That's how old the ghost story is.

One final question: Do you have a favourite ghost story? There are many. These are some of my favourites.

So, let the journey begin by turning the first page. Then read on, but do look over your shoulder from time to time.

Author's note

*M*ost of these stories were passed on to me by Maritimers who appreciate the art of storytelling. Many have kept a record of grannie's folklore; others remember hearing the stories as children over a flickering candle or kerosene light.

In some cases, I have taken storytelling liberties where subtle embellishment is like frosting on a cake, but I never stray too far from the heart of the tale. Included are a few stories from my own disturbed imagination.

My profound gratitude to all those wonderful people who invited me into their homes, where many hours were spent listening to and recording these wonderful stories for my *Maritime Mysteries* series on ATV.

And to those busy folk who took advantage of coffee shops, shopping centres, Canada Post, the telephone, e-mail, and faxes, to share with me their favourite ghost stories, I am forever grateful.

Chapter One

Haunted Homes and Halifax Haunts

Penelope

*T*slow my pace—even stop—when I'm passing Shirreff Hall on the corner of South and Oxford Streets in Halifax. I'm constantly reminded of the young woman whose ghost may still be roaming the corridors of Shirreff Hall, a home away from home for female students attending Dalhousie University. The young lady in question was a domestic by the name of Penelope.

During my research for the *Maritime Mysteries* series, an editor of the campus paper told me that there are no records in the University's files on this young woman's employment. It's as if she never existed.

Was there ever a Penelope? Or was she—is she—merely the creation of a too-vivid imagination of young impressionable students? I will tell you what was told to me, then you can decide for yourself.

Back in the late twenties, Penelope worked as a domestic on the third and fourth floors of Shirreff Hall. When she didn't show up for work one morning, a thorough search of the residence was made. She was found in the attic, hanging from a rope. At the time of this writing there is still a piece of that rope, albeit rotting and frayed, still hanging from an attic beam. Perhaps it's still there. And perhaps it's the same rope Penelope used to hang herself!

What terrible event drove Penelope to take her own life? And what powerful forces keep her restless spirit walking the corridors of Shirreff Hall?

The reasons for taking her own life are still being discussed by Dalhousie students in the late hours of the night. Not long after she committed suicide, some students saw her ghost wandering the fourth floor. Some of these students, with a frightened look in their eyes, reported that while studying, a sudden wave of cold air swept over the room and they had a strange feeling that someone had just walked into the room. Others, awakened from a sound sleep by some force, tell of a young woman standing at the foot of their beds. When they ask her who she was, she vanished. And there are still other students who speak of the presence of an unexplained force that is beside them when they walk down the long, dark corridor to the bathroom. Others speak only of an uneasy feeling of being constantly watched.

Is it really the ghost of Penelope? Scoff if you may, but don't try to tell the students I talked with that they were seeing things, or that they were letting their imaginations run away with them. As far as they're concerned, Shirreff Hall is haunted—haunted by the ghost of Penelope.

Even now when I walk by Shirreff Hall I wonder if Penelope is watching from a fourth-floor window. I want to look up, but dare not, just in case.

The Ceilidh Spirits

*H*is car broke down on a lonely stretch of road that appeared to go nowhere. Should he stay in the car where it was safe, or walk to the nearest village and put up for the night? The thought of a warm bed was the deciding factor.

It was near midnight when he saw a light up ahead. His pace quickened toward the house he saw. When he opened the gate and walked to the front door, he heard music coming from inside. His knock was answered by a old woman. He told her he was stranded and asked if she would she be so kind as to give him shelter for the night. She invited him in and he followed her to the kitchen, where she pointed to a chair at the table—all the while humming the tune the group was playing in the other room. She suggested he should have his tea in the parlour, where he could enjoy the singing and dancing. He sat down in a comfortable old sofa and admired the talent of the young musicians. There were seven in the band altogether; four men and three women, and it was plain to see they were all related—perhaps brothers and sisters. They were, without exception, handsome young people. And all, except one, had wavy, jet black hair. The tallest and thinnest young woman had hair the colour of a golden sunrise.

What he found disturbing and a little peculiar was that they neither spoke or acknowledged his presence. It was as if he didn't exist. He couldn't help but feel somewhat uneasy. And the room itself, while warm and friendly, had a foreboding air about it.

Sleep overcame him, and he lay down on the soft warm sofa. The last thing he remembered was the old woman covering him with a blanket whilst in the distance, he heard the soft, strains of "Dark Isle."

When he opened his eyes in the morning he was startled to find himself lying on a cold and damp floor! The room that had been so warm was now cold and empty. The fireplace that only hours earlier had given off such warmth was closed off. There wasn't a single piece of furniture in the parlour or in the kitchen, nor was there another human being in the house. Slowly he made his way up the winding staircase to the rooms upstairs. The only thing he found was an overgrowth of cobwebs and a sickening and musty odour in the empty rooms.

He quickly went downstairs and out the front door into the bright sunshine and onto the road that seemed to go nowhere. He had gone less that a kilometre when he saw an old man coming his way. His steps, supported by a cane, were slow and deliberate. Should he tell the old man what he had seen, or didn't see? He thought better of it. No sense being laughed at, or worse, thought of as a fool. They nodded to each other and moved on.

The repairs to his car would take most of the day and evening. While eating dinner at the local diner, he noticed on the wall a newspaper headline: LOCAL MUSICIANS AND GRANDMOTHER DIE IN TRAGIC BUS ACCIDENT. The story carried a family picture; the familiar faces of the young musicians and the old woman who had given him shelter the night before stared back at him.

He was about to turn onto the main road when he changed his mind. He felt compelled to go back to that place, to make sure. It was midnight when he saw the lights come on, and as he drove off, music came pouring out of the abandoned farmhouse.

The Witches of Robie Street

You don't believe me, do you? You don't believe there's a haunted house on one of Halifax's busiest streets. May I suggest you get in you car and drive by? Or, better still, walk by. If you have the courage, linger awhile. But I caution you, don't linger too long, because on the verandah, the Witches of Robie Street may still be dancing the dance of death. If they catch you spying on them ... well, don't say I didn't warn you.

The city of Halifax is famous for many firsts. It was home to the formation of the first representative government in the British colonies, and the first newspaper in Canada was published here. What's that got to do with haunted houses? you may ask. Well, the house in question was built in the 1840s for William Caldwell, the first elected mayor of the city. The home, known locally as the Robie Street Palace, has changed hands several times. And the spirits? Well, who's to say they're not still there.

The house is currently a combination of a residence and clinic. Patients waiting to see the doctor may choose from a variety of magazines available; the curious will reach for a small five-by-seven white card that explains the history of the Robie Street Palace and how it became haunted, and that its mysterious black window is what made the place so famous.

According to legend, one evening, just at dusk, an old man living in the house was caught spying on three witches who were performing a ritual dance on the verandah. The witches became very angry and put a curse on the old man, and the window he was spying through was turned black by these angry souls. To this day it is said that no matter how many times the glass is replaced, it immediately turns black.

The early residents who lived in the Robie Street Palace were witness to some very mean-spirited poltergeists. For no apparent reason, lamps would suddenly go hurtling across the room, doors would slam shut and then swing open again, and very late at night, voices were heard groaning in the dark upstairs.

On closer inspection of the now boarded-up blackened window, it's difficult to tell what colour the glass really was, or is, or if there really was a window there at all.

Some southenders who know the history of the Robie Street Palace pass by quickly—they've heard about what may happen if caught staring.

The Mystic Farm Ghost

Just off highway 101 there is a place known as the Jordan Branch Road, which is located not far from Shelburne, Nova Scotia. There you will find the Mystic Farm. The house was built in 1783 and is currently owned by Jack and Jill Nickerson, who operate a greenhouse nursery.

Life appears normal at Mystic Farm. Normal, that is, until night falls. That's when the ghost of Nina appears. Nina, according to the new owners, was one of the original owners, who lived into her ninety-ninth year.

The young couple first realized the home was haunted when early one morning, Jill was going downstairs to get a glass of water. When she was halfway down, she felt a foreboding and a sweep of ice-cold air passed through her body. Jill knew instinctively that a spirit had passed through her. When she turned to look up the stairs, she saw the shadowy figure of an old woman disappear into a spare bedroom. The next morning, Jill began exhaustive research about the farm and its previous owners, and especially about the ghost who now occupied their home. What surprised the Nickersons was that they were just the second owners of the farm. For 215 years, the place was owned by just one family—the last to live and die there was a woman called Nina.

Nina made her presence known in several ways. It was just after two o'clock one morning when Jill was awakened by the smell of smoke. She and her husband rushed about the home checking every room but couldn't find any fire. After airing out the house and returning to bed, with the smell of smoke still hanging in the air, the young couple knew there would be no sleep that night—Nina was on the prowl.

Contending with one ghost is one too many, but the Nickersons had to deal with two: one inside and one outside. The second spirit never entered the home or appeared to anyone; it's presence was known only by a steady knocking on the back door. The knocking first happened one day when Jack was working around the home while Jill was away. Even when Jack opened the door, the knocking continued. No matter what he did in an attempt to get rid of the knocking—from ignoring it to turning up the stereo—nothing worked. The knocking only became more persistent and louder.

When the Nickersons investigated further, they discovered that some years earlier, a young man was killed when his vehicle smashed into a large boulder on their property. Apparently, the young man's ghost was knocking on the door trying to get help.

The Nickersons are somewhat philosophical about the ghosts that have returned to (or never left) Mystic Farm. As Jill Nickerson put it with a smile, "They're part of our family—or we're part of theirs."

The Tancook Spook

One of my more memorable Maritime trips was a visit to Big Tancook Island, located in Chester Basin, Nova Scotia. I was producing a television program about the island and its people. It was an unforgettable experience because of the generosity and friendliness of those wonderful Tancookers.

One afternoon, I was invited up to the wheelhouse of a local boat, and the conversation eventually got around to Maritime Mysteries. I was asked if I was familiar with the story of the Tancook Spook. I came away with a wonderful and humorous story of one pesky spirit.

Most everyone at one time or other has experienced how pests in the home, if not eradicated, can get out of hand. But what about a persistent and pesky ghost who's making your life miserable? How do you get rid of that? Do you call in a ghost exterminator? Well, if you live on the island, you call for the services of a Tancooker who has a sure fire old-world method of getting rid of those unwanted spooks. His method, however, isn't foolproof. You'll forgive me if I take license in the telling of this story, as I've heard at least half-dozen versions. This is my favourite.

There once was an old man who lived alone, until one day, an unwelcome and unannounced guest arrived. This old gentleman didn't even know the intruder was in residence until one night he was awakened by some awful noises coming from the attic. "Damn," he thought, "racoons must of gotten inside." But when he went up to investigate, there were no animals and nothing was disturbed. The old man was no sooner back in his bed when the racket started up again. Only this time, the noise sounded like it was coming from the kitchen. But when he went downstairs to check, he found nothing out of the ordinary. The old man didn't return to bed, but sat up next to the kitchen stove until dawn, thinking about his problem and if his house was haunted. Every night was the same. He became a victim of some ghostly pranks, including the slamming of doors, and heavy footsteps on the stairs. The last straw came the night he heard whispering at his locked bedroom door. Next morning, he went to see the one person who could tell him how to get rid of the ghost once and for all.

The information the old man was given had nothing to do with seances, burning candles, prayers, or holy water. All he needed was an oversized potato sack, a shovel, some patience, and a lot of luck.

Around eleven o'clock, the old man retired for the night and deliberately left the bedroom door open. He held the potato sack in his hands, hidden under the blankets, and waited in the dark. He had been told that when a spirit enters a room the air around the spirit is icy cold and there is also an odour. Sometime after midnight, he heard footsteps coming along the downstairs hall. He held his breath and waited. The footsteps were now on the stairs. The old man's heart began beating faster and faster. If it didn't slow down, he was sure he'd have a heart attack and the ghost would have won; would have gotten him out of the house for good! He was sure that's what the ghost wanted.

Suddenly, he felt a chill go through him, and there was a distinct change in the air. He was certain the ghost was now in the room. He could also smell a peculiar odour. Suddenly, from the left side of the bed, cool air swept over his face. Was the ghost now standing over the bed looking down at him? It was now or never. With one incredibly fast motion, the old man threw off the blankets, raised his arms high, and where he believed the ghost to be standing, covered the spot with the potato sack. He couldn't believe it! The sack was jerking so hard, he could hardly hold it. It was as though the bag was filled with snakes! The old man quickly tied the bag with a strong rope. While he got dressed, he watched as the ghost inside the bag tried to get loose. He was surprised how light the bag was when he flung it over his shoulder and went outside. There, he picked up a shovel and headed into the woods in back of his home. He remembered what his friend told him—find a spot that is isolated and dig a deep hole and bury the sack. That will be the end of the ghost. When he was finished, he patted down the earth with the shovel, tipped his cap, and went back home to bed. When he woke up the next morning, he was refreshed. It was the first good night's sleep he had had in weeks. However, the best laid plans often go awry, and in this case, that's exactly what happened.

About a month after the old man buried the ghost, a group of young people on the way home from a party came across the newly dug ground. They wondered if someone had buried something of value, or perhaps even a corpse! Full of false bravado, they began digging until they uncovered the potato sack. They looked at each other and smiled. It took a while before they got the knot around the sack untied. When they finally opened it, all that came out was a puff of foul air.

At the exact moment the sack was opened, the old man was awakened abruptly by an angry voice screaming curses. He heard dishes being smashed and the sound of angry footsteps coming upstairs! He knew at once that the ghost was back.

The Unseen Ghost

One day not so long ago, I received a letter from Cynthia Sharpe of Cow Bay, Nova Scotia, telling me a fascinating story of what happened to her and her family after they purchased a century-old home. There is, for me at least, something fascinating about an older home; and at the same time something foreboding. It's as if I expect the place to be haunted. Not all are, of course, but Cynthia's is.

When buying one of these ancient dwellings, you never know exactly what's included in the purchase price, until you live in it for awhile. That's what happened to the Sharpe family. Nothing appeared out of the ordinary, everything was as it should be, until one evening while Mrs. Sharpe was wrapping Christmas gifts in her bedroom. Her dog was lying at her feet. The closets in the home have the old fashion latches that must be lifted to open. No one else was in the room and there was no one in the closet—no one human, that is. Suddenly, the latch on the closet door lifted and the door opened. When the dog looked toward the open closet door, her fur stood on end and she flew downstairs. That was the first indication that there was something in the home other than human beings. Cynthia says the closet door may remain unopened by human hands for days, even weeks, but will suddenly fly open and slam shut all day.

At other times, houseplants are tipped onto the floor.

During the Christmas holiday of 1996, for example, the family was seated in the living room when a Boston fern was overturned. The pot was smashed to pieces and dirt spread all over the floor and curtains.

No one, including the Sharpes, has ever seen the spirit. Cynthia says there are times when she believes she sees something. To get to the door, visitors must pass in front of the picture window first. Cynthia says when she's watching television she'll sometimes catch glimpse of someone passing by the window and she'll tell her husband they have a visitor. But when he answers the door, there is no one there.

There were many other strange happenings: once the handle on the stove flew across the kitchen floor. Cynthia was relieved that her mother-in-law saw this happen, and that she was not the only one to witness such things. Another time, a loud noise shook the whole house. When Cynthia went upstairs to check, she found her childhood sleigh, which usually stood against a bedroom wall, upside-down in the middle of the bedroom floor.

The incident that scared Cynthia the most happened one day when she was working in the kitchen. Suddenly, the washboard she had mounted on the wall exploded. Cynthia says she was putting leftover food in containers at the kitchen table and had taken a few steps to the refrigerator when she heard the explosion of glass. When she looked down, there were several shards of glass where she had been standing moments before.

Is there an explanation? Cynthia says she hasn't one. So why do the Sharpes stay? Cynthia says so far no one has been hurt, and she feels that whomever, or whatever, it is, just wants everyone to know they're not alone in the old home.

The Uptown Ghost

Parkerhouse Inn stands a step back from the busy sidewalk on Sydney Street in uptown Saint John, New Brunswick. It was built on the grand scale of the Victorian influence, and it has a history of undying love and ghostly manifestations. If you feel a cold breeze as you walk by 71 Sydney Street, there's a good reason for it. Here's why.

In 1890, a Saint John doctor, Walter Woodsworth White, built a magnificent home for his bride to be. Ah, but love at times is fickle. The beautiful young maiden changed her mind. He was too old, she said—all of 28. In time, however, she changed her mind and three years later they were married and moved into their honeymoon mansion. They had three children and lived happily into their later years until the good doctor died. The grieving widow was devastated. The mansion became a cold, lonely, and empty place without her beloved.

The widow acted on impulse and sold their beautiful home, but as the years went by, she regretted her decision and longed to be back at 71 Sydney Street. Her wish came true, but not in this life.

Today, Parkerhouse is operated by Kathy Wyatt and Gary Golding. Aside from the regular paying guests, the innkeepers believe they have a non-paying one—not of flesh, but of spirit. And they also believe the apparition is the good doctor's wife. Kathy Wyatt questions how else one could explain the extraordinary things that have been happening in their newly acquired home. There is, according to Kathy and Gary, a sense that there's another dimension within the mansion, and that someone or something is living in that space.

The first incident happened with a spinning wheel that was owned at one time by Mrs. White. Just three days after the new owners moved in, they were seated in the den discussing the day's activities, when for no apparent reason the spinning wheel began turning. A quick check of the whereabouts of the family confirmed there was no one near the wheel. There have been other incidents that convinced Kathy and Gary they are not alone in the home. A second unexplainable incident happened while Kathy's mother was visiting over the Christmas holidays. She was suddenly awakened when her body rolled over to the other side of the bed. It was as if someone had sat down on the edge of the bed, there was no one in the room at the time. No one can convince Kathy's mother that she was dreaming or seeing things. Something did sit on the bed! That she was certain of.

Gary Golding is the type of person who does not accept anything quickly, especially anything about the paranormal. However, seeing is believing, and Gary firmly believes that something spiritual has taken over the inn. As he put it, "It is a feeling that aside from us humans, there's another presence in the home." Kathy agrees, and adds hastily, "The ghost is a kindly soul, a motherly type." And she knows when the ghost is near—her dog, K-C, senses the ghost's presence first and bids a hasty retreat.

The Ghost Burner

*B*efore buying that older home, there are things you should consider besides the possibility of a leaky roof or damp basement. You should also inquire about the history of the property. Who owned it originally, who died in it, and under what circumstances.

This is the story of one old curmudgeonly ghost who just wouldn't stay where he belonged—in the ground. When he was alive, he had agreed to give his neighbour first refusal on buying his homestead when he and his wife passed on, providing his daughter, living in the U.S., wasn't interested. The daughter wasn't interested, and honoured her father's promise to sell to his neighbour.

The only reason the neighbour wanted the home was to get control of the land so he could keep developers out.

It wasn't long before the new owner's son moved in. It was an ideal place to study—no interruptions to contend with. Little did he know that someone else had also moved in, or had never left. That someone else was a mean-spirited ghost who was about to make the young man's life miserable.

The new tenant was no sooner settled in for his first night's sleep when suddenly he heard the sounds of heavy footsteps coming up the stairs. He sat up in bed thinking perhaps it was his father coming to check on him. But it wasn't. It wasn't anyone, but he knew there was something at the top of the stairs—perhaps now even in the bedroom. Needless to say, the young man kept the light on in his bedroom for the rest of the night.

Next morning, he crossed the road to his father's home and told him that the house he had bought was haunted. When the father merely smiled and spoke of people with vivid imaginations, the boy invited him to spend a night in the old house. The challenge was quickly accepted by the father. Again, no sooner were they comfortably in their beds that night when they heard a creaking sound from somewhere downstairs, possibly in the hallway. They then heard footsteps on the stairs, and a scraping sound, as if someone was dragging their nails along the wall. Neither realized that the ghost was in their bedroom until the window was slammed shut. Father and son spent the rest of the night with the lights on, staring at the closed window. Both agreed in the morning they would figure out a way to rid the place of this late-night intruder.

How does the ghost-plagued dweller get rid of something from the other side? People have tried everything, from seances to exorcism. But there is yet another way: a sure-fire ghost-burner. While sipping his morning cup of coffee, the father smiled as the answer to the ghost problem came to him. He imagined the old ghost was also listening, but powerless to do anything about it. That brought another smile to his face. "This is what we have to do to get rid of the ghost," he told his son. "We have to find some old clothes the ghost wore while alive and burn them—shirt, pants, shoes, overalls, anything." There was nothing of the old man's left in the house, but hanging in the barn they found a pair of overalls and a plaid shirt. The father instructed his son to place the clothes on the ground and then pour kerosene over them. The father struck a match and dropped it on the soaked clothes.

Gone for good? One doesn't know for sure whether the burning of the old man's clothes actually sent him back to his grave. Perhaps his spirit was merely carried on the flames to the neighbour's attic where he is biding his time, waiting for the perfect moment to return to his old haunts…

The V.I.P. Ghost

*B*uilt on Hollis Street in 1862, the Halifax club is one of city's oldest landmarks. It is a staid and quaint club, where the likes of Sir Charles Tupper and Sir Robert Borden sipped afternoon tea. A list of the original members of the club reads like a city street map, Almon, Binney, Cogswell, Creighton, Cunard, and Uniacke to mention just a few. No one knows if the ghost that haunts the place today is one of those builders of the city and country. According to the few employees who have seen him, or think they have, he's a slow and deliberate ghost, prowling every room as if in search of someone. There have been many stories as to who he is and why he's haunting the place. The most popular one tells of the untimely death of one of the more prominent members who died in the arms of a lady of the evening. She promptly removed him from her boudoir and had him dumped on the doorstep of the club.

Like it or not, the gentlemanly ghost will continue to haunt the old place until he finds what he's looking for. Until then his presence will be felt in this comfortable old-world atmosphere.

The McFarlane Ghost

*T*his ghostly tale began in 1965, when the McFarlane family rented the old Ford home on Bridge Street in Sackville, New Brunswick. The family consisted of John McFarlane, a physics instructor at Mount Allison University, his wife and four sons.

The McFarlanes enjoyed living in this stately old mansion until they discovered that a spirit from the 1870s was living with them. This unnerving discovery was made by their youngest child, Andrew.

Andrew would regularly tell his parents during breakfast that sometime during the night a strange-looking woman had stood by his bed and whispered "There, there, my child you will get better, the doctor is on his way." Or she would sit on the edge of his bed and stroke his forehead in a soothing manner.

For a time, Andrew's mother dismissed it as nothing more than a vivid imagination. That was until one morning, while making Andrew's bed, she was overwhelmed by a strong lavender odour, a scent she never used. Mrs. McFarlane slumped down on the bed. She felt a power controlling her, and knew she was not alone in the room. She sensed that someone was there close by, perhaps even sitting next to her. When she gained her composure, she immediately left Andrew's room and went directly down to the kitchen. She was now convinced that what Andrew told her was much more than a child's fertile imagination.

That evening, Mrs. McFarlane told her husband what had happened and that she believed their home was haunted. Unless he found a way to get rid of the ghost, she insisted that they would have to move. Mr. McFarlane called on the services of a local medium, who recommended a seance that might identify the spirit and its reasons for haunting the home. Andrews's older brother David witnessed the seance and remembers what the medium told him after he came out of the trance: "While I was in a trance, the ghost, speaking through my body, spoke of how bitterly cold it was; how much frost was on the windows. Then the tortured spirit, in a mournful voice, spoke of how her child had galloping consumption." The medium also told the McFarlane family that while in the trance, he had seen people hurrying in and out of the child's bedroom and he was certain one of the people was the doctor. He then said the ghost, in great anguish, had told him of her son dying in her arms. The spirit blamed herself for her son's death.

The medium concluded that Andrew's room had been that of the spirit's child, and that the spirit kept returning to comfort the boy. That was no relief to the McFarlane family—they moved.

The Law House Ghost

There is a home in Gagetown, New Brunswick, that was built in 1863 by a John Law and is to this day known as the Law House. It is haunted.

As of this writing, the home is owned by John Stewart. John's late wife, Ann Stewart, kept a journal of her life in the Law House, in which she describes her first impressions of the home: "The last rays of the afternoon sun cast a feeble gleam across the field where remnants of dusty snow lay." Mrs. Stewart also wrote of the day when she and her husband visited the home with the landlady, and she encountered an apparition. It happened as Mrs. Stewart and her dog, Suzie, were walking down the hallway. Suddenly, the dog stopped and refused to go any further. "What is it girl? Do you see a mouse?" Ann Stewart asked. She bent to pat Suzie's head to reassure her, when she felt a cold chill sweep up her spine, making her hair stand on end. When she looked up, she saw a spectral light outlining a figure or form. The vision was clear for the thirty seconds in which she and Suzie stood transfixed, then it moved toward the back wall. Ann followed the disappearing figure, trying to discern how on earth it could travel through the wall.

When she returned to the living room, the landlady noticed something strange about Ann.

"Did you see a ghost?" asked the owner.

"No, no I didn't *see* one" responded Ann. "I felt something. There is definitely a presence in the back hall."

The owner then told Ann that when she had lived in the house and whenever she was ill, the ghost would appear at the side of her sickbed. It seemed concerned over my well-being," she explained.

There were other encounters between Ann and the spirit of Law house. She believed the ghost would fulfill any and all her wishes— perhaps the spirit knew what Ann was thinking.

Ann had a friend by the name of Rosemary, whose company she very much enjoyed. Rosemary became very special to Ann because of an incident that was much more than a coincidence. One cold and damp morning, the telephone rang and Ann fumbled into her housecoat and hurried down stairs to answer it. As she was running downstairs she lamented aloud that she wished she had a shawl." I could grab a shawl quickly and wrap it around me instead of trying to get into my housecoat and wasting time," she thought.

The next day, Rosemary came by and over her arm she carried a shawl. Ann and her husband looked at each other with wide eyes. "Did you ask Rosemary for the shawl?" her husband stammered.

"No, I didn't," Ann assured him.

"I was about to put this is the Salvation Army box that we keep at home for old clothes," Rosemary told them, "but for some reason I thought you might like it."

"I like it very much," Ann told Rosemary, thanking her. She hung the shawl on a peg in the hall where it remains to this day. The shawl for Ann was a kind of symbol of faith. A coincidence? Ann thought otherwise.

Ann does not name the spirit anywhere in her journal. There are speculations of who the ghost might be; some previous owner, perhaps, or a lost soul. Today, Ann's husband, John, lives alone in Law House. Well, perhaps not entirely alone.

Chapter Two

Restless Spirits and Unfinished Business

The Ghost of Lucy Clark

She was waiting for me on the banks of the old mill damn. Her legs were tucked up close to her chest, arms folded around her knees. She was rocking back and forth. Something inside told me to turn and run; something else was pulling me toward her. When I came closer, I noticed her hair was so long it touched the ground. And when she beckoned me to sit by her, her hair was the only part of her that seemed alive. The skin on her face and hands was the colour of slate. It was difficult to tell her age, no more than sixteen, perhaps even younger. She was wearing a long white dress.

When she turned toward me, her head moved in a jerking motion, and she kept her neck hidden from me by deliberately letting her hair cover the left side of her face. There was something she didn't want me to see. When her eyes—deep set and lifeless—met mine, a chill went through me. The smell of death was all around her. I wanted to run, but couldn't. Something I can't explain kept me there. When she spoke, a deep, rasping whisper came out of her throat: "My name is Lucy Clark."

Lucy Clark! My blood ran cold! Lucy Clark has been dead for over a hundred years and the story of her appearances are still told in every household in the village, and for a hundred miles beyond.

I will put down all the facts of this story as I have heard them, so in your own time and wisdom, you can decide for yourself whether the story of Lucy Clark came out of a too-fertile imagination or a bad case of indigestion. If, in the end, you're still not convinced, then go down Londonderry way and ask the good folks there. See what they have to say.

The first time Lucy Clark came back from the grave was on the old Cumberland road, the route the stagecoach travelled between

Truro and Amherst, Nova Scotia. This incident occurred in the community of Lornevale, tucked in between the regions of Londonderry and Folly Mountain.

This is the way the story unfolded:

A handsome team of six horses were harnessed and ready when Ned Purdy, the stagecoach driver, came out of the depot and climbed aboard. He cracked the whip over the heads of the two lead horses and the coach moved out of the depot yard and onto the old Cumberland road. The horses kept up a steady gait and the passengers were reasonably comfortable. It was a warm summer evening with little or no wind to speak of. There was nothing out of the ordinary, nothing that is, until the stagecoach rounded the first sharp curve on the road. The lead horses bolted almost pulling Ned off his seat. Standing in the middle of the road was a woman wearing an ankle-length white dress. "Who the Hell..." Ned blurted out. When he got the team under control and looked up the road again, she was gone. Was his imagination playing tricks on him? But what spooked the horses? Sometimes a bear or deer crossing the road can set the horses off. Perhaps that was it, thought Ned. He was about to sit down, when out of the corner of his eye he saw the woman standing just below his seat, blood oozing from a torn jugular in her neck. She was reaching up with outstretched arms. Fear took hold of him, but it was a fear that also made him whip the horses on. Ned Purdy didn't know it at the time, but he was the first to encounter the ghost of young Lucy Clark.

It was some years later before Lucy's ghost appeared again. This time it was to Tom Adams of nearby Westchester. One day, Tom decided to exercise his dogs on the old Cumberland road. He had heard many times Ned Purdy's story about his encounter on the same road with the ghost of Lucy Clark. It's not that Tom didn't believe the story, he just wasn't thinking about it on that day.

Tom and his dogs were no more than a quarter of a mile into their walk when it happened. Coming toward him in the middle of the road was a woman in a flowing white dress. Tom shook all over as a chill went through him. The whimpering dogs backed away. Tom Adams then remembered the story of Ned Purdy's experience with the ghost of Lucy Clark. He knew that if it was Lucy Clark, it was too late to run. She was now upon him, walking quickly—or rather more like floating than walking. Her arms were outstretched, and when she spoke her voice was but a rasping whisper: "My name is Lucy Clark and I beg of you not to be afraid; not to run off like the others have. You must listen to me—hear why I cannot rest in my grave until the truth is known. It is said that I was carried off by a bear. That is not true. I was murdered! Murdered by the hand of my own brother!" Tom was in a state of shock; he was frozen. The ghost began telling the tragic tale of her death. "One day, my mother and father left my brother, Frank, and me, to care for the farm animals while they were away for the day. Sometime after supper, our prize pig got out of his pen. My brother had a mean temper and he screamed at me to corner the pig, but the pig was too fast. In a fit of rage, my brother grabbed an axe and struck me across the neck—he killed me. Frank then took my body to the old mill dam. He let the water run out of the dam, and then buried my body under large stones. He then let the water flow back in. When my parents returned home late that evening, he told them a bear had carried me off into the woods. My parents and the authorities believed his story. If you tell what really happened, I will be free and my soul will forever rest in peace."

Tom Adams was unable to speak; he could only nod in agreement. Lucy Clark then vanished before his eyes. When Tom Adams returned home he collapsed from the ordeal. It took several weeks before he could bring himself to talk about what Lucy Clark's ghost revealed to him that evening on the old Cumberland road.

Tom Adam's grandson, Arden Mattix, confirms his grandfather's encounter with the ghost of Lucy Clark. What she told Tom about the way she died was confirmed many years later by her brother, Frank, who, on his death bed, confessed to the murder of his sister and revealed where the body was buried. When the authorities drained the old mill dam, they found the skeletal remains of Lucy Clark!

I began this tragic tale by telling you that Lucy Clark was waiting for me on the banks of the old mill dam. Well, yes, but only in one of my many recurring dreams—or nightmares.

The Lady in the Blue Dress

This is not one of those "a long time ago" ghost stories—it's a 1990s tale.

When the story of the Lady in the Blue Dress came to my attention, I immediately set off for Indian Harbour, Nova Scotia, where this sad tale unfolded.

Sitting behind the wheel of my car as I approached Peggy's Cove I noticed how abruptly the landscape changes. There's a sparseness to the land. It falls away to a flatness and disappears behind a seawall of boulders that keep the pounding surf at bay. Above the high cliffs, the steeple of a church rises above the tiny cluster of houses that dot the landscape.

On the whitecaps, a lone Cape Islander was barely visible against the rays of the sun. And above the village, a fluttering of gulls left the sanctuary of the church steeple and flew off to circle above the incoming vessel. They would circle high above and wait until buckets of fish-waste were thrown over the side and then they would fold their wings and dive.

When I arrived at Indian Harbour, I met with two of the principals involved in this remarkable story. One was the daughter of the Lady in the Blue Dress and the other was Donna McGuire, an artist, and the owner of Rogues Gallery.

I've changed the family name of the Lady in the Blue Dress to avoid any embarrassment to those distant relatives who may still be living in the area. Here, then, is the story of the ghost who walks the rocks of Indian Harbour.

It was destined to happen. No one could prevent it, least of all Marlana, a popular Toronto radio psychic. Marlana was looking forward to a holiday in Nova Scotia with her friend Donna Cameron. A few days after Marlana arrived, Donna decided that she, her two children, and Marlana would head for Indian Harbour to visit her good friend, Donna McGuire.

Sometime after arriving at the McGuire's home, Donna Cameron decided to explore the rugged shoreline with her son. In the meantime, Marlana went on a driftwood hunt with Donna's daughter, Christine.

When they returned, Marlana asked Donna McGuire if there was a legend in the village about a woman who was seen out on the rocks. Donna looked somewhat puzzled and told Marlana that she had never heard of such a legend. Marlana pressed on, "Nothing about a woman in a blue dress?"

"No," Donna replied, "Nothing like that." Everyone now became interested in why Marlana was so concerned. What was the reason for her questions.

There was a long silence. All eyes were on Marlana. She then told them what happened. "When Christine and I arrived at the shore, I was suddenly overwhelmed by a feeling of loneliness. I didn't mention it to Chris, but told her that I didn't like the place. And then I had this feeling that I had come to Indian Harbour from Scotland, and that the people here didn't like me. As we moved closer to the high rocks, the feeling of loneliness and separation grew even stronger. Suddenly, a woman in a long blue dress appeared out of nowhere. She stood on the rocks staring. Then, as quickly as she appeared, she vanished. I didn't mention what I saw to Chris. However, on the way back I saw the woman again. I felt certain she was trying to make contact with me; trying to tell me something."

When Marlana finished her story, Donna McGuire suggested they she should visit Hattie Sutherland, the oldest resident in the village. If anyone knew of a legend and a strange woman seen on the rocks, it would be Hattie. They were received warmly by Mrs. Sutherland, and nothing would do until the traditional afternoon tea and cakes were served. Marlana waited for the right moment, then told Hattie of her experience on the beach and what the woman she had seen looked like. There was a moment of silence as Hattie listened while sipping her tea. "The woman you describe sounds like the stories I've heard about my mother. She came to Indian Harbour as a war bride from Scotland. I'm the youngest of five children and was far too young at the time to remember very much about my mother and what happened to her. According to what I've been told, though, it wasn't long after she arrived in Indian Harbour that she was not accepted by her in-laws. I suppose they were bitter over their son marrying someone from overseas. Anyway, it was a difficult time for her. My father was a fisherman, and he spent long periods of time at sea. It was a lonely time for my mother and she would stand on the rocks and stare out to sea as if she was trying to will herself back to Scotland.

"When my father drowned during a storm, his family cut off all contact with my mother. Now alone and lonely, she wrote to her father begging him to come over to Indian Harbour and take her back to Scotland. My grandfather did come over, but either couldn't support, or didn't want anything to do with her children, so we were left behind in the care of relatives. To this day I don't know what was on my mother's mind. Perhaps she thought that in time, we'd all be together.

We never heard from her again; never knew if she was alive or dead. Then, one day a letter arrived from Scotland informing us that she had died. Those who knew her in Scotland said she took the guilt of leaving her children behind to her grave. Maybe that's why she came back. I mean her ghost, that is."

What Hattie Sutherland told Marlana and Donna McGuire is pretty much the same as what she told me.

If there is a postscript to this ghostly tale, it's this: surely Hattie Sutherland must wonder why her mother's ghost has yet to make contact with her.

If ever you go down Indian Harbour way, walk the rocks if you must, but before you leave visit Rogues Gallery and say hello to Donna McGuire, the artist who captured the Lady in the Blue Dress on canvas; a tragic, lonely, and ghostly figure.

Mrs. Copeland's Ghost

There's much more to Sable Island than natural gas—a lot more. There's the ghost of Mrs. Copeland. This is her tale of woe.

Sable Island is located some 350 km southwest of Halifax, Nova Scotia. The salty Maritime Mystery that takes place there involves a shipwreck, a murder, and a bleeding ghost.

There are at least two versions to this 18-century mystery that we know of; both are partly fact and partly fiction, although some fishermen will say the story is completely factual. One version, nearly as old as this story, was written by the author of *Sam Slick*, Thomas Chandler Haliburton, and the more recent one, *Fatal and Fertile Crescent*, was written by Lyall Campbell. Of course, there are countless oral versions, and folklore always also plays a significant roll in Maritime Mysteries.

So let the journey begin, to a place of broken ships and restless spirits. A ship laden down with the personal belongings of the Duke of Kent set sail from England in 1799 for the garrison town of Halifax. Among the passengers were a Mr. Copeland—the garrison's doctor—his wife, two children, and a maid.

When the ship failed to arrive in Halifax, the Duke sent out a search party to look for it. The first obvious place to investigate was Sable Island. When the search party arrived on the island, they found the beach strewn with debris, including many of the Duke's personal belongings. There were also the victims of the shipwrecked vessel. The officer in charge told his men to bed down for the night and they would bury the dead in the morning. In the meantime, he would check the other side of the island for any survivors.

There were, at the time, small huts on the island built specifically for survivors of shipwrecks. Realizing it was getting late, the officer decided to stay in one of the huts and return to his men in the morning. He lit a fire then went outside again to continue searching for survivors. When he returned to the hut, there was a woman standing by the stove. Her long white dress was dripping wet and soiled by sand and seaweed. When he asked who she was and where she came from, she held out her left hand. Her ring finger was missing and oozing with blood. When he moved closer, she fled past him and out the door. He followed and watched her flee over the dunes until she disappeared. When he went back inside, she was again standing by the stove. It was then he recognized who and what she was. It was the ghost of Mrs. Copeland, wife of the garrison's doctor! That was the last time he saw Mrs. Copeland—or rather, her ghost.

On his return to Halifax, the young officer promised himself that he would avenge Mrs. Copeland's murder by seeking out her murderer and returning her ring to her family in England. As soon as he arrived back in Halifax he went after the most notorious member of the wreckers gang—a local group known to prey on victims of shipwrecks. While talking with the daughter of the man he believed to be Mrs. Copeland's murderer, the woman told him that her father found the ring on the beach on Sable Island. The child's mother, however, said that a Frenchman, on Sable Island at the time, had given the ring to her husband. She added that if he wanted the ring back, he could buy it from the local watchmaker. In the end, he did purchase the ring and kept his promise to the dead Mrs. Copeland by returning the ring to her family in England. However, her murderer was never caught. According to those living on the seedy side of Halifax, he suffered a worst fate than the gallows. In his sleep the ghost of Mrs. Copeland would rise up to point an accusing and mutilated finger at him.

Fishermen who sailed close to Sable Island at the time reported seeing a shadowy figure, with an outstretched hand, staring out to sea as if waiting for the return of something ... perhaps a finger and ring!

Ashley's Encounter

This incident occurred in a small community outside of Sheet Harbour, on Nova Scotia's south shore. It came my way by the brother of the sister involved, and by the sister's insistence, the names have been changed.

It was a cold winter's afternoon in the late 1930s when Ashley finished school for the day and headed for the safety and warmth of her home. The route she travelled never varied. Her only concern was passing the local graveyard. When the cemetery came in sight, her footsteps always quickened.

On this particular day as Ashley reached the main gate of the cemetery, she was startled by a tall woman coming toward her from between the tombstones. Young Ashley was terror-stricken. She wanted to flee, but was unable to move. She could hear only the beating of her heart. There was snow on the ground, and as Ashley would later recall, the woman left no footprints in the snow, nor did she open the locked gate. She simply walked through it. The stranger took Ashley's hand, and led her away from the cemetery.

When Ashley opened the back door of her home and stepped in the kitchen, the smell of cooking filled her nostrils. Her mother greeted her with a smile, a cup of warm cocoa and hot tea biscuits.

"So," her mother asked, "how was school today?"

"Okay, I guess," Ashley replied. Then staring off as if her mind was elsewhere, she told her mother that she met a woman by the graveyard on the way home from school. "She walked a ways with me before leaving. She wanted to know my name and what grade I was in and which school I was attending. She also said that when she was a girl, she went to the same school." Ashley's mother was anxious to know the name of this stranger. "She knew you," Ashley said, "she went to school with you. She said her name is Grace Forshaw."

"No, Ashley," her mother exclaimed, "the woman you met was not Grace Forshaw. Grace Forshaw died twenty-five years ago!"

The Ghosts of Uniacke House

*W*hy did Martha Uniacke return from the grave? And why did her daughter join her in eternal vigilance?

Many people leave this world whimpering and afraid; afraid of death, the unknown, and the darkness. And most never return. The answers as to why this mother and daughter returned may lie in the mansion itself and in those who lived there.

Mount Uniacke was built in 1813 as the country home of Richard John Uniacke, Attorney General of Nova Scotia. Uniacke named the estate after his ancestral home in Ireland, where his family were prominent and prosperous members of the landed gentry. Uniacke was born in 1753 at Castletown, Ireland.

Following a bitter quarrel with his father, he set sail for the new world to seek his fortune.

He arrived in Philadelphia in 1774, where he met Moses Delesdernier, a Swiss resident of Nova Scotia who was in Philadelphia seeking residents to settle in Nova Scotia. Delesdernier liked Uniacke and convinced him to come to Nova Scotia and work for him. Uniacke agreed, and the following year at age 21, he married the not yet 13-year-old Martha Delesdernier, daughter of his employer.

On my first visit to Mount Uniacke, I was overcome by a feeling that time was suspended; that the people who once lived there, and died there are still there, in spirit. As I got closer to the mansion, I had an uneasy sense that I was being watched from behind musty smelling drapes. Once inside, I was certain of it. I was also aware of a sadness. The imposing portrait of Richard John Uniacke, the master of the house, hangs on the hall wall and those piercing eyes of his never leave you.

Martha Delesdernier, who bore Uniacke twelve children, died at age forty. It wasn't long after she passed away that strange things began happening. Field workers and house staff noticed Martha wasn't where she was supposed to be—in her grave. What happened in that mansion to bring her back from the graveyard? And why did the spirit of Lady Mary Mitchell, Martha's eldest daughter, also return from the dead? Both Uniacke women are sometimes seen arm in arm strolling down by the lake. Other times they are seen inside the home, and at times, Lady Mitchell sits at the piano while her mother sits and listens. They do not appear to be upset, nor do they attempt to convey a message to the living.

Martha and Lady Mitchell go about their mysterious ways even when tourists from many lands and cultures visit Uniacke House. Most visitors are unaware of the ghosts. But as Goldie Robertson, the Chief Heritage Interpreter, reminded me, there are those who have a special insight into these things—they feel a presence of something or someone from beyond. Such was the case with a family visiting from Lebanon. They were about to enter a bedroom on the first floor when the mother gasped and withdrew from the room. She quickly gathered her children around her and left, telling the guide the room was haunted by two women. The frightened visitor told the guide one spirit was sitting on the bed, while the older lady was seated in a rocking chair.

There is little else to be said about why these two 18-century ladies who haunt Uniacke House; until and unless they somehow convey to the living why they are not at peace in their graves, it will remain a Maritime Mystery.

Next time you visit Mount Uniacke, look beyond the obvious. You'll never know what might be watching from the top of the stairs or staring back from behind the hemlock.

The Man They Hanged Twice

*H*e was taunted by relatives, and picked on by his friends. They told him that he had to get even with the man who took his woman. So, young Bennie Swim swapped his guitar for an old .38 Smith and Wesson and set off on a murderous journey in a place called Benton Ridge, New Brunswick.

It was March 27, 1922, sometime around four o'clock in the afternoon when Bennie knocked on the back door of the farm house where his pregnant former girlfriend lived with her new husband. The husband answered the knock, and he was shot dead in his tracks. Bennie then turned the gun on his old girlfriend and shot her in the chest. When she tried to run, he shot her a second time in the back and she fell to the kitchen floor dead. Bennie then turned the gun on himself, but the bullet that lodged in his head did little damage and he survived to face the hangman's noose.

The first words out of his mouth when the sheriff caught up with him were, "Sheriff this is awful, I suppose I'll hang for it." And he would. Not once, but twice!

Bennie's last days were spent behind the bars in the Woodstock, New Brunswick, provincial jail. According to guards, Bennie was a model prisoner.

During his preliminary hearing, a plea of insanity was entered by the defense. Many witnesses testified that young Bennie Swim was insane. A Government psychiatrist, however, found him mentally competent to stand trial for the double murder. When it was over, the jury found Bennie guilty of first degree murder and he was sentenced to hang on July 15, 1923.

There were, according to reports, several volunteers wanting the hangman's job. Some even came from the state of Maine, willing to do the job for a price. The sheriff who was responsible for hiring a professional hangman was having a difficult time getting an experienced one. Because of that, the hanging was postponed twice. The country's top hangman, Arthur Ellis (not his real name) was otherwise engaged; no doubt hanging other Canadians. Finally, two Montreal hangmen were recommended—a poor recommendation for Bennie Swim. They were little more than amateurs who had gained their so-called experience hanging blacks in the southern United States.

Seven months after the murders and at approximately 5:00 P.M. on Friday, October 6, 1923, Bennie Swim was led up the steps of the provincial jail in Woodstock to the gallows. While Bennie Swim prayed, a black hood was placed over his head and the noose placed tightly around his neck. Bennie was still praying when the trap door was sprung. A few short minutes later, an unconscious Bennie Swim was cut down. There were three physicians in attendance. To their surprise and horror, they found that Bennie was still alive! On further examination, they also discovered that Bennie's neck wasn't broken in the fall—a sure sign of a bungled hanging. No one outside of that examination room will ever know if Bennie actually regained consciousness. According to those in attendance he never did.

Bennie was carried back up to the gallows and hanged a second time. Bennie hung there for some twenty minutes before he was cut down and pronounced dead. His body, but not his spirit, was placed in a cold grave by relatives.

An official investigation into the bungled hanging was held. Witnesses testified that the hangmen were drunk. No blame was placed on the local sheriff for selecting the two hangmen from Montreal, but it was recommended that future hangings should be carried out in a federal penitentiary by professionals. This was not the last that would be heard of the botched hanging of Bennie Swim.

Sometime later, guards at the jail reported hearing shuffling footsteps and doors being slammed shut. Other times, and especially late at night, a voice was heard moaning as if in pain. Did the ghost of Bennie Swim return to the Woodstock Jail?

We do know that new guards are told by their superiors how to cope with that restless spirit during the midnight hour: keep busy, read a book, or listen to the radio.

All the guards agreed that whatever the ghost did, he did twice. A coincidence?

The Jailhouse Mystery

Built in 1840, the Charlotte County Jail in St. Andrews, New Brunswick, was operational up until the 1970s, when it was turned into a museum of sorts. What makes this old jail different is that it has a resident spirit—a ghost that is.

In the nineteenth century, the prison population was made up mostly of petty thieves, the homeless, alcoholics, and debtors. There were, however, a few hardened criminals who passed through its steel doors, including a few unfortunates, such as Thomas Dowd and Eliza Ann Ward of New River, New Brunswick.

It was in the fall of 1878 when Dowd and Mrs. Ward were transferred from New River to St. Andrews, where their murder trial would be heard. The good folk of St. Andrews went about their business until the trial started. Once it got underway, it was standing room only.

Dowd was convicted of the axe murder of Eliza Ann Ward's husband, Thomas Ward. Mrs. Ward was convicted as an accomplice, but as she was pregnant at the time, was spared the gallows and was sentenced to seven years in prison instead. Some believed the child she carried was Tommy Dowd's. Dowd maintained his innocence throughout the trial, but in a later confession wrote, "I killed Ward in the valley where he was found. I killed him with McCarthy's narrow axe. Ward was on his way home with an axe and pitchfork. When we met we had some words. He made at me with the fork. I clinched the axe and killed him. I then took him by the legs and dragged him to where his body was found. Mrs. Ward never saw him after he left the house; till she saw him dead in the woods, nor anyone else but myself." This confession, some say, was prompted by Mrs. Ward's condition. Apparently, he wasn't aware at the time the court had spared her life.

While awaiting the hangman's noose, Dowd returned to his faith and spent most of his waking hours praying.

On the morning of January 14, 1879, with a priest and guards on either side, Dowd was taken from his cell and lead to the awaiting gallows. Mrs. Ward was allowed to watch the hanging from a jail window. Witnesses reported that she was weeping when taken back to her cell.

According to records, Mrs. Eliza Ann Ward died shortly after serving her sentence. Found in her personal belongings was a letter. In it she confessed to the murder of her husband!

In time, St. Andrews returned to normal. However, things at the jail were anything but. Guards reported strange sounds during the night and a mysterious beam of light would appear on the wall along which Dowd had been held. Guards reported that it was as if an invisible hand was trying to write a message. Another guard said it was Dowd's ghostly hand that scrawled the words, "I'm innocent!" that appeared there.

The Ghost of Kelly's Mountain

*I*n the cool morning air a lone loon is heard as it skims over the water of the Bras d'Or lakes. The mist rises from the forest floor and sweeps over the mountain, but the peace and serenity is broken by a voice that is hurled back down the mountain, "Ye keep that bloody stuff off my mountain, ya hear!"

It's the voice of a spirit that's filled with Irish fury; it belongs to Patty Kelly, a crotchety old Irishman who claimed the mountain as his and his alone.

Kelly was a true mountain man living in isolation. Old Patty had good reason for keeping the curious out; it's said that he made his own whiskey and moonshine, and didn't want anyone discovering where his stills and booze were hidden.

Even in death, Kelly swore he'd return to guard his mountain against anyone attempting to trespass on or deface it. When old barley corn finally caught up with him, he passed away, but not his spirit—it stayed on the mountain to watch over what was his.

When workers on the new Trans-Canada highway reached the mountain, it was obvious to everyone that what was happening was being done in the name of progress—everyone that is except Patty Kelly. His antics frustrated workers, who couldn't figure out why their heavy equipment was constantly breaking down. Others complained of a strange old man who suddenly appeared out of nowhere, forcing their vehicles off the road. And when workers came on shift in the morning, their tools were strewn all over the place. In the end, some suggested the mountain was haunted. Ultimately, however, progress won out. The Trans-Canada Highway over the mountain was finally completed.

On the east side of the mountain toward Seal Island Bridge, there is a treacherous curve in the road—a favourite place for the Kelly ghost to suddenly jump out in front of cars, nearly sending driver and automobile over the mountain and into the lake.

One day, a driver and his passengers, who were on their way home from a Ceilidh, witnessed an old man in overalls and a plaid shirt doing a jig on top of the mountain. If it was Kelly, he must have been sampling his barley corn. One motorist even reported seeing a man in the middle of the highway who ran toward his car and passed right through it! These stories reached nearly every home on the island, including that of Charlie MacKinnon, who immortalized Patty Kelly and his mountain in a popular folk song.

So, an Irish fable? Maybe, yet when I drive over Kelly's Mountain, I feel like I'm being watched. Next time you're driving over it, keep your eyes open, because you never know who's watching, or running alongside your car—and keeping up!

The Hitchhiker Ghost

This story was told to me in a check-out at a local grocery store by a young woman who said it was one of her father's favourite ghost stories.

I later came across a similar story in Janet and Colin Bord's *Unexplained Mysteries*. Either version raises the hair on the back of your neck. If you're ready, lets put the Harley in gear and see what's over the next rise.

The night sky was an explosion of stars when the young biker said goodbye to his girlfriend and headed down the highway. He lived by a fast rule—never stop for a hitchhiker unless it was an emergency. So why did he stop for the young woman who seemed to appear out of nowhere? It's as if he didn't have a choice. He waited until she strapped on the extra helmet before heading back down the highway. Some miles later, he felt her release his waist. When he pulled over to check, the young woman was gone. However, the helmet was strapped securely to the seat.

When he arrived at the next town, he told several waitresses in a fast food restaurant what had happened. They listened politely, and when he had finished his story, they told him that what he had experienced was nothing new; that other drivers had had similar experiences.

One such driver was a middle-aged man, who stopped his car for a young woman one night, and after driving some fifteen minutes, turned to speak to her but she was gone! He reported what had happened to the police, and his story was reported in the press. That story was read by a man who claimed his girlfriend was run over and killed in the same location. When the driver of the car was shown a picture of the young woman, he confirmed she was the one he had given a ride to.

So, next time you and your Harley are out for a pleasant drive and you feel as if someone has just put their arms around your waist, well...have a nice ride!

The Roundhouse Ghost

This story is by way of Leo Evens of Sydney, Nova Scotia, a retired Sydney and Louisburg railroader, and somewhat amateur historian of the Whitney Pier area of Sydney. In my teens, I too worked for the now defunct S&L.

We're told you can never go back. You can, of course, but nothing remains the same. Your favourite corner store where you bought those juicy honeymoon candies when you were a child was probably torn down to make way for a strip mall. People grow up, leave the old neighbourhood or die. It all changes eventually.

The only things left of the Sydney & Louisburg Railway are memories and ghosts. The buildings are gone, nothing left but rusting rails and grass that has gone to seed.

It was in 1942 and the height of the war, when I was offered a job on the railroad. Most of the able-bodied men had gone into the service. At the time, my father was an engineer there, which is probably why I was hired.

I remember my first day on the job. I was nervous, and wanted very much to make a good impression. I even remember the foreman's name: Joe R. Macdonald. We would eventually become good friends. My shift was midnight until 8:00 A.M. Joe R. explained to me and another worker what our duties were. Just before he left for home, he said, "Oh, by the way, ignore the ghost. He won't bother you." We thought at the time he was joking. He wasn't.

From that moment on, and whenever I was at work, I kept looking over my shoulder and dreaded the times I was alone. If I was, indeed, alone.

There were many theories about why the ghost was haunting the place, but no one ever found out. As one railroader put it, "When you come face to face with a ghost, you just stand there with your mouth wide open. You want to scream, but nothing comes out."

The ghost's presence was first noticed by two employees who were working the graveyard shift. They were standing just inside the large open doors of the roundhouse, watching a light snow coming down. Something moving in the cab of an engine caught their attention. Who could it be? they wondered. There were no other workers around, and the first crew wasn't scheduled until 6:00 A.M. Something else bothered them. Why were there no footprints in the snow leading up to the cab of the engine? When they climbed aboard to investigate, the cab was empty.

The ghost's favourite place was near the workbench. He'd stand between engines observing the men working. That led some to believe he must have been a foreman.

One of the more frightening encounters happened when a callboy, or dispatcher, was alone in the office. While the boy was on the phone, the door opened and the ghost walked in. The callboy wanted to run, but he was to scared to move. He knew if he stood up his legs would collapse under him. All he could do was sit there and watch the spectre move around the office. Then as quickly as he came in, the ghost turned, stared at the startled young man for a moment, and left.

To this day, the legend of the roundhouse ghost persists, and although the railway and buildings are long gone, some, like Leo Evans, believe the ghost is still there, moving in the tall grass where the roundhouse once stood.

The Pipe-smoking Ghost

*T*here are people who, when entering an empty building, feel an energy and instantly know they aren't alone. Gloria Burbidge found out through some mysterious clues that her two-hundred-year-old Brooklyn, Nova Scotia store is inhabited by something other than humans: objects are often not in their proper places, doors that were locked securely for the night are found open in the morning—and most mornings when Gloria arrives at the store, there's a heavy odour of pipe tobacco in the air.

Gloria and close members of her staff didn't speak of what was on their minds for quite sometime, but it soon became readily apparent to everyone that what was happening wasn't the work of a prankster, but a genuine ghost. So, with a country sense of humour, they christened their resident ghost Hector. Whenever something fell from a shelf, everyone would nod in agreement. Hector is about.

In an attempt to get to the bottom of this Maritime Mystery, Gloria called on the talents of two psychics, who both spent a considerable amount of time touching and smelling things on the first floor. But when Gloria took each psychic up to the attic on separate occasions, it was a different matter. The first psychic spend only a short time in the room and said the energy and force there was so heavy she had to leave. The second psychic didn't make it to the attic. She didn't even get to the top of the stairs before collapsing in an emotional state. From their reaction, it was obvious Hector was in the attic. The second psychic told the owner that she had a vision of someone being thrown down a flight of stairs. According to local history, there is a story that there was a tavern located upstairs in the store over a hundred years ago, where, the story goes, a man was killed when he was thrown down the stairs.

To this day, a beverage salesman will not go into the storage room alone. A couple of years ago he was checking supplies when he suddenly felt something strange near him. When he recovered from the shock of whatever it was, he told the staff that he hadn't seen anyone, but a pungent odour had overwhelmed him. He said he would quit his job before he'd go back there alone again.

Gloria recalls another incident when a young man planned on staying in the store overnight to raise money for a rock-a-thon. No sooner had he settled in for the night when a ghostly and shadowy figure crossed in front of him.

Whenever customers step inside the Brooklyn general store, they're greeted warmly by Gloria Burbidge and her staff, Some sniff the air— the familiar smell of pipe tobacco is everywhere. They nervously steal a glance towards the stairs that go up to the attic, wondering if the ghost of Hector is coming down…

Chapter Three

Sea Stories

Jerome–A Man of Mystery

*T*he tides of the Bay of Fundy wash against the Digby shores and leave behind familiar, and sometimes strange and peculiar, flotsam and jetsam, but nothing as strange as what two fishermen found early one morning in the mid 1860s.

The day before the discovery, local fishermen watched intently from the deck of their vessels, from the shores and houses of Digby Neck, as a mysterious ship sailed back and forth close to the coastline. It was not like any ship they had ever seen. They agreed that it must be from some foreign land. That night, discussions at their supper tables revolved around why this mystery ship was staying so close to the Digby shore.

The next morning, two local fishermen were walking along the beach at Sandy Cove and may have unknowingly solved the mystery of the ship that had stayed just offshore the day before. What they found was a strange-looking man, perhaps in his mid twenties, sitting in the sand with his back against a large boulder for support. When they got closer, they noticed that his legs were gone. The remaining stumps just above the knees were wrapped in blood-soaked bandages. The fishermen attempted to communicate with the stranger, but he did not, or could not, speak. They realized if he didn't receive immediate medical attention, he would surely die.

The two men carried the stranger to the Gidney home, not far from where he was found, and immediately put him to bed and provided him with medical attention. Officials questioned the stranger as to his identity and asked how and why he ended up on Sandy Cove Beach. It was evident from the start that any attempt to establish a dialogue with this man of mystery was futile. The only word he uttered sounded like "Jerome." From that moment on, he was known by that name only.

It was decided that perhaps if he were sent to the Acadian region of the bay, someone there may be able to converse with him in his own language. It was thought that because of "Jerome's" dark complexion, he was perhaps either Italian or Portuguese. The logical home for him, then, would be in Meteghan with the Nicholas family. John Nicholas was a Corsican who spoke several languages and certainly would have great empathy for this pathetic-looking young man. Nicholas fought in the Crimean war, he was captured, then escaped, and made his way to Nova Scotia and found a new life within the Acadian community.

Nicholas felt certain that Jerome understood Italian. When he spoke to him in that language, he could see a reaction to his questions in Jerome's eyes. During one period of questioning, Nicholas thought he heard a word from Jerome that sounded like "Trieste." One thing was clear to Nicholas—this mystery man was living in great fear.

In the months to come, Jerome's health improved and he was able to move around on his stumps. He spent many hours sitting on the cliffs looking out to sea. What was he thinking? Was he expecting a ship to come and rescue him? Or was he afraid that someone out there on the high seas was coming to murder him?

Jerome's stay with the Nicholas family lasted for seven years, but when John Nicholas's wife died, Jerome was forced to move in with a Mrs. Dedier Comeau of St. Alphonse de Clare, then known as Cheticamp. At the Comeau home Jerome settled in quickly and instantly became friends with the Comeau children. According to the children, when the adults were out of the house, he would speak to them, but would fall silent again when the older folk returned. Once, the children asked him why he wouldn't talk to grownups, and Jerome shook his head, saying, " No, no." And when the children asked him how he lost his legs, he said, "Chains. Sawed off on table."

The government of Nova Scotia paid for newspaper advertisements in the hope that someone might know the identity of Jerome. As a result, many people visited the Comeau home, but for the most part, these people were merely curious and only wanted to look at the mysterious "Jerome." The government notices even reached the Mahoney family, living in New York City. The two Mahoney sisters wrote the Comeaus, thinking that Jerome might be their brother who had run away from home when he was eleven years old. The Mahoney family had spent their life savings trying to locate their lost brother. In the end, however, it turned out that the Digby County Jerome was not the Jerome of New York City. Many other theories about Jerome's identity were proposed. It was even suggested that Jerome was a ward of the province of New Brunswick, and that to avoid paying for his keep, New Brunswick officials had had him dumped on the shores of Nova Scotia.

Many of the children who had known Jerome when they were young visited him when they returned to Clare. On one of these visits, a young woman asked Jerome several questions about the early days and if he remembered her. When she begged him to speak, he raised his old head and simply said, "Je ne peu pas."

When Digby County's mystery man was found on Sandy Cove Beach he was around twenty-five years old. He lived in that area for over forty years and when he died in 1908, he carried to his grave his name, the name of his country, the reason for his legs having been amputated, and the answer to the mystery of his abandonment on that beach so long ago.

The Ghosts of Devil's Island

Located at the mouth of Halifax Harbour is a barren and treeless piece of land called Devil's Island. It lies there, desolate, with only the wind and ghostly voices of the past sweeping over it.

During World War II it served as a military lookout and blockade against Germany's U-Boats. Before, and in between the two world wars, it was home to a dozen families who were all fisher folk, and all highly superstitious. From its past come stories of hoofed strangers, forerunners, haunted houses and drowned fishermen.

If I was to do justice to this story I needed to get on the island; to feel for myself what it was like now and what it must have been like back then. Unfortunately, access isn't that simple. There are no wharves to ease your boat up against; you either swim from a boat anchored off shore, or use an inflated rubber boat, such as a zodiac, to run straight up on the rocky beach. As you move in from the beach, walking can be difficult in the knee-high grass. The island is a pot mark of deep holes; some call these holes rat nests. And watch where you step, the place is a graveyard for sea gulls.

Standing by itself on the island is what remains of an abandoned home—gutted by time, weather, and people. Some say the last resident of this home was the island's caretaker. What happened to all the others homes? At its peak, there were over fifty people living there. Standing there in the middle of that desolate place one can imagine hearing above the wind the voices of children at play. Where are they now? And do they still remember the way it was? Do they remember stories the old people told of forerunners and ghosts—like the story of Henry Henneberry? Am I standing where old Henry stood? Is his spirit still here? Perhaps in that abandoned house.

Henry was a young fishermen who went out on the sea at sunrise to cast his nets. His wife stood in the kitchen window overlooking the waters below, and saw her husband wave from his boat. What she didn't see was Henry taking a wrong step, falling overboard, and drowning. While this happened, Mrs. Henneberry was going about her housework upstairs. At the exact moment her husband fell into the ocean and drowned, Mrs. Henneberry heard footsteps in the kitchen. She thought it strange to be hearing the footsteps of her husband! Why was Henry back so soon, she wondered. When she went downstairs, however, there was no one there. But there were wet footprints left on the wooden kitchen floor. Henry, it is said, was no sooner in his watery grave, when he rose up and came home to his beloved wife.

When old Mrs. Henneberry passed on and her children moved away, another Henneberry family, who scoffed at such things as haunted houses, moved into the old Henneberry homestead. One evening, young Mrs. Henneberry was sitting in her rocking chair with her infant daughter, Henrietta, in her arms. The young wife and mother kept her gaze on the ocean watching for her husband's boat. But what came in from the sea that evening was not her husband, Dave, but an ill-wind. Fishermen told her that her husband had stumbled and fallen overboard. His body was never recovered. During her short stay on Devil's Island, the young widow heard the voice of her husband calling for her to join him. Not long after his tragic death, young Mrs. Henneberry became gravely ill and soon died. When family and neighbours returned from the graveyard, they found the infant daughter, Henrietta, who was a happy and healthy child, also dead!

The island folk gave the Henneberry house wide berth when they passed by. It remained empty for a long time. There were several reports of people seeing the ghosts of Henry and David Henneberry in their oilskins moving about the old homestead.

Some islanders thought they had the solution in ridding the island of the haunted Henneberry homestead—they decided to tear it down board by board. That was a mistake, of course. The island families that used the wood from the Henneberry home lived to regret it. Their homes became new homes for the Henneberry ghosts!

To this very day, the granddaughters of Henry Henneberry have never set foot on Devil's Island and because of what has happened there, never will!

The sea-going Coffin

One of the strangest Maritime Mysteries I know is the story of a coffin that washed up on the shores of Prince Edward Island. The waters that wash against these shores hold forever the secrets of this strange tale.

The person that was inside that coffin was Charles Coughlan, an actor of the late 1800s. He was tall, handsome and had a magnetic personality; the John Barrymore of his day. There are no available records of exactly where he was born. Some say Dublin, others, Paris. Some loyal Islanders claim him as a native son.

He and other American actors of the Broadway stage often vacationed at Bay Fortune, Prince Edward Island—a popular summer retreat for artists. Charles was the centre of that famous colony of creative types and the darling of everyone, especially the ladies. A rapscallion of the first order, some would have said.

While appearing on a Galveston, Texas, stage in 1899, Charles Coughlin was suddenly stricken by a fatal illness. Against his wishes, to be buried at Fortune Bay, Coughlin was buried in a Galveston cemetery. The following year, 1900, a violent hurricane swept in from the Gulf of Mexico, destroying everything in its wake. The flood waters that followed not only washed away homes, but also the cemetery, sending hundreds of coffins into the gulf, including Coughlin's.

The currents of the gulf carried Coughlan's coffin up the Florida coast and eventually into the waters of the Northumberland Strait, where the currents, or some unexplained power, carried it into Fortune Harbour, a distance of two thousand miles! Coughlan was home—eight years after having been swept into the gulf!

Two fishermen hauled the coffin onboard, and saw the nameplate: Charles James Coughlan 1841–1899. In the end, Charles Coughlan got his wish and was buried on his beloved Prince Edward Island.

The Phantom Ship of Northumberland Strait

There are many unexplained mysteries that, I expect, will remain so. And there are, on record, several accounts of these mysteries, including that of the phantom ship that was, and is, seen from the Bay of Chaleur to the Northumberland Strait and many waters in between. Numerous witnesses have testified that they have seen this nautical phenomenon.

Of all the accounts of phantom or ghost ships, the burning ship seen plowing the waters of the Northumberland Strait seems to be the one most frequently reported. With that in mind, here's one version of the tale of the phantom ship that sails ever eastward.

Some time during the year 1880, a local fisherman, for no apparent reason, lifted his eyes from the shore and looked out over the strait. There, riding high on the water, was a three-masted schooner.

Puff-like flames climbed the rigging until the whole ship was eventually engulfed in fire. The fisherman watched the burning vessel as it sailed at a high speed in an easterly direction. Suddenly it was gone—it vanished as if into thin air. Actually, as would later be reported, it had plunged beneath the frigid water.

Ernie Rankin, a life-long resident of Pictou Island, remembers the first and only time he saw the burning vessel. He was sitting in his favourite chair, looking out of the kitchen window. Ernie smiled when telling me what he saw on the Strait. "I was just a little boy and I remember it was at night and all the family were outside in front of the house looking southeast—watching the burning ship. I remember it was a mass of flames."

Another witness of the phantom ship is Margaret McMaster of Caribou, Nova Scotia. Margaret sighted the ship in 1939 while on her honeymoon. "You could see fire shooting up from the mast," Margaret exclaimed, "but we didn't see any bodies on it like some have reported. It was moving in a southeasterly direction and sailing on the tide. It was eerie, alright." Margaret also remembers hearing the story of rumrunners who were racing across the Strait with a full load of liquor. The rum boat was sailing in the wake of the phantom ship and the captain and crew decided once and for all to unravel the mystery. So they staid the course and sailed right into what Margaret described as a rosy phosphorus-like glow. The crew then realized they had sailed right through the ghostly vessel.

Margaret McMaster is not the only member of her family who has seen the phantom ship. Her son Ed witnessed it as a young boy. He and his companion were bicycling one evening when they were astounded by the illumination over the waters of the Strait. When I sat down with Ed, he told me that what he had seen was hard to explain: " It was different from anything I had ever seen. There was fire, but no smoke. You could see the flames leaping up the rigging. We got the hell out of there quick as we could. It was an eerie experience, I tell you."

Is there an explanation for this phantom ship phenomenon? Could it be likened to St Elmo's fire—a flame-like electrical phenomenon seen in the rigging of ships and along the wings of airplanes? There have been several theories put forth, but none that can satisfy or change the minds of those who have seen the phantom ship.

Some believe the ship is the *Fairie Queen* that sunk in a violent storm in 1853.

Who really knows for sure. What we do know is that the phantom ship of the Northumberland Strait will remain, until proven otherwise, one of the Maritime Mysteries of all time.

The Woman in White

*M*any Maritimers are familiar with the story of the phantom ship that burns while sailing over the waters of the Northumberland Strait, but what about the woman in white who is seen standing on wind-swept cliffs of Nova Scotia's Pictou Island? Is there a connection?

Those who have seen the burning ship have also reported seeing the woman in white at the same time. They say that her arms are outstretched as if reaching for some lost soul aboard the doomed ship. Some believe that she is the lost soul.

Pictou Island is about five miles long and two miles wide. There is only one road on it and it runs the length of the island. The island itself is some ten miles from the mainland of Nova Scotia. At one time, there were about thirty families living on Pictou Island, who made their living by way of the sea and land. Most of the young people are gone; they left for mainland opportunities. Today, there are but a handful of people left and they are mostly elderly.

While visiting the island a few years back, I sat in Ernie Rankin's kitchen and listened to his stories of long ago; stories of his youth and of the only time he saw the burning ship of Northumberland Strait. His eyes sparkled and a slow smile spread across his broad and friendly face when I asked if he had ever seen the woman in white. "No," he said, "but I know of a young man who did. I won't tell you his name because of what happened to him—it would embarrass the lad. It was dark when this young man was walking home one night along that lonely road. Suddenly, out of nowhere, the woman in white appeared before him. The young man, half scared out of his wits, ran. When he got home he collapsed." That encounter sent the young man to the hospital in Dartmouth with what Ernie Rankin described as a complete mental breakdown.

There are also fishermen who claim to have seen this spectre of the night. While sailing by the island, some claim to have seen her in her flowing white dress with outstretched arms, standing on those high cliffs. Other fishermen tell a more compelling story of their encounter with the apparition. While tending their nets on the shore, they saw a tall, young woman in an ankle-length white dress coming toward them. They stood silently watching as she walked past them and into the Northumberland Strait and before the men could reach her, she disappeared beneath the water. The fishermen stood there dumbfounded, when suddenly, a bright light appeared over the water where the woman had vanished.

As if hypnotized, the fishermen then watched as a great and flaming ship rose up out of the turbulent waters and sailed in an easterly direction. As quickly as it appeared, the ship sank below the waves.

The Maritime Mystery question to ponder: Does the woman in white have anything to do with the burning ship? I asked Ernie Rankin that question. He sat there, rocking in his favorite chair, looked at me, and smiled. Then he turned his head toward the waters of Northumberland Strait. Waiting, watching, and smiling.

The Ghost of Petpeswick

*T*his is a spirited tale of a British soldier who wanted to go home in the worst way. Unfortunately for him his posting was Halifax, Nova Scotia. In the summer of 1835, a convoy of British troop ships en route to Halifax was caught in a violent storm. Most of the ships were driven off course. One waited out the storm in Petpeswick Harbour. The homesick soldier who stood in the late afternoon shadows of the vessel slipped over the side and began the long swim to shore. It was not to be. He was spotted and was ordered to return to the ship. When he refused, the young deserter was shot. A boat was lowered and four soldiers rowed to where the body was floating. On orders from their superiors, they buried the body in an unmarked grave. That evening, the troopship pulled anchor for Halifax.

Many years later, the Young family decided to build their home on land overlooking Petpeswick Harbour, where the body of the British soldier was buried in an unmarked grave. Unknown to the family was the fact that the property, the woods behind their home and the waters of Petpeswick Harbour were haunted by the spirit of the young British soldier.

Not long after the home was finished, and the family had settled in, they became aware that things were not normal. Doors were being opened and closed on their own, and heavy booted sounds could be heard coming in the backdoor, going through the hall, and out the front door. What the family didn't realize was that the ghost of the young British soldier was walking through the house from his unmarked grave to the waters of Petpeswick Harbour.

There were other incidents in days to come that would convince the family that their home was haunted. If tools were not locked away, they would disappear. And then, one day, a new sound was heard.

The Young family and neighbours were awakened by chopping sounds in the woods. When they investigated, no one was found, but they did hear heavy breathing and the familiar sounds of a tree being felled.

As suddenly as the ghostly activities started, they just as suddenly stopped. The family were relieved, but couldn't help but wonder what had happened to the ghost. When the Youngs turned to their wise old grandmother, she smiled and said, "He's gone back to England. That's why the haunting and the chopping in the woods stopped." When they asked what she meant by that, she said, "Don't you see, the chopping stopped because he finished building his ghost ship. He's sailing home, back to England."

A Seagoing Mystery

While spending a vacation on Cape Breton Island, I spent some time travelling up north. One day, while enjoying a coffee and sandwich at a local eatery, an elderly gentleman introduced himself and apologized for the intrusion. "That's okay," I told him. He then proceeded to tell me about his adventures sailing around the world and wanted me to know that ships like houses are also haunted. I agreed. Was I interested in hearing a tale?

Of course.

"Well, then," he said, "I'll tell you one—one you've never heard before." He was wrong, I had heard it before; I heard it the first time while on Big Tancook Island and again in a fisherman's shack at Three Fathom Harbour. The story is also included in Helen Creighton's *Bluenose Ghosts*.

As it's impolite to tell someone you've heard the joke or story before, I listened as this salty old salt proceeded to tell me one of his favourite sea-faring tales.

"There was this Captain George Hatfield, out of Fox River, Nova Scotia, and this happened well over a hundred years ago. Anyway he sailed out of Cuba bound for New York and ran into a bad storm. Well, sir, after riding out the storm for near two days and two nights he was exhausted and needed to get some sleep. So, after giving orders to his first mate, he went below to catch forty winks. No sooner was he asleep, when somebody was trying to wake him up, and the capt'n heard a voice whispering, 'Keep her off half a point.' Well, sir, this kinda set the captain off a bit so he went topside to tell the mate off. But the mate told him it wasn't him. Anyway, ol' Capt'n Hatfield went back to his bed wondering if a dream could be that real. Well, he fell asleep again and damn if it didn't happen again. There it was. Someone tapping him on the shoulder and telling him, 'Keep her off half a point.' Up to the bridge straight away went a really mad capt'n. And again the mate told him no one went below and that he must be dreaming. Back to his bed goes Capt'n Hatfield and sure enough no sooner was he asleep when again someone was nudging his shoulder. This time it was not a whisper he heard, but a command to keep her off a half point. When he opened his eyes, there was this stranger leaving the captain's cabin. Capt'n Hatfield noticed the clothes he wore were different from what he and his crew wore. Back on topside he asked the mate and crew if anyone saw a stranger leaving his cabin. They told him they saw no one. Then he remembered the voice in his sleep, so he told the mate to keep the ship off half a point. He then went below and slept the rest of the night. Next mornin', ol' Capt'n Hatfield told his crew to keep a sharp lookout. It didn't surprise Capt'n Hatfield when they came on a vessel in trouble. Now this other captain was a fellow named Amesbury. And his ship was named the *D. Talbot*. On board were Amesbury's wife and two children. They were brought safely aboard Hatfield's vessel just before the *D. Talbot* sank.

The survivors told Capt'n Hatfield it must have been a miracle he was in the same waters as they were. Well, sir, Capt'n Hatfield thought about that for awhile and then told them about the voice in his dream telling him to alter course and keep her off half a point. When he described the stranger leaving his cabin, Captain Amesbury's wife, nearly fainted away. When she got her breath back, she told capt'n Hatfield the man he described was her father who had died ten years ago!"

When the gentleman finished his story, he smiled and said, "Well, how about that."

I smiled and said, "Yeah, how about that." We said our goodbyes and before he left, he said he'd send me some more mysteries of the sea and some landlubber ones as well. I'm still waiting.

The Ghost of Chebucto Light

A young girl walks her dog along a path at Chebucto Head Light. The animal cowers, sinks low to the ground and growls. His black eyes focus on something moving over the high cliffs. The girl also sees it. Her body stiffens, fear sweeps over her. What is in the distance is not whole, it takes no definite shape; it is transparent, floating over the rocks like a ghost. A large bonnet covers most of the face—if there is one. It wears a grey dress, cinched in at the waist, and flowing outward and down to the ground. And there is a rope tied around the thing's waist. As suddenly as it appears, it vanishes. The child quickly returns to the safety of her home. Her parents listen to her story, but laugh it off, telling her there's no such thing as a ghost.

The young girl's name is Pat Flemming. Today her married name is Helpard and she is an educator. Chebucto Head Light is located at the entrance to Halifax Harbour. When all this happened, Pat's father was the lighthouse keeper.

For all of her teen years, Pat felt there was someone or something trying to make contact with her. Most nights, while waiting for sleep, there was always a strong, unexplained presence in her room. She now believes it was the ghost she saw on the cliff who was trying to communicate with her, and that the rope tied around the ghost's waist indicated only one thing—she was the victim of a shipwreck. Perhaps during a violent storm the woman's husband had lashed her to the ship's mast to keep her from being swept overboard, but in the end, she drowned, and her ghost is wandering the cliffs of Chebucto Head in search of loved ones.

Pat's father was a firm believer in the here and now and nothing in the hereafter. That is until one evening, while in his boat, a stranger appeared above the high cliffs. "What in the hell is that?" he whispered. Stan Flemming saw a tall woman wearing an ankle-length dress floating down the side of the cliff. In disbelief, he watched it float past his boat and over the water until it disappeared. Whatever it was, Stan knew it wasn't human. That's when he became a believer.

When the lighthouse was eventually automated, the Flemmings were forced to move. For a long time, the home remained abandoned.

One day a radar technician knocked on the Flemmings' door. He had a story to tell. He told them that one evening during a winter storm, he was forced to stay overnight in the empty house at Chebucto Head. Sometime during the night, he was abruptly awakened when his portable cot was overturned and his alarm clock was smashed against the far wall. He left, fighting the storm, rather than facing the unknown.

Teazer

*A*mong those many islands in Mahone Bay there are, from time to time (but not recently) reports of a flaming ship that sails over the waters, then dips it bow and disappears beneath the sea. Is it the phantom ship *Teazer*, or merely the imagination of those who wish to believe. Perhaps it's a combination of moon reflection, fog banks, and island shadows, and bored fishermen wanting to tell a tall sea tale. Regardless, there have been many sightings and those who have come forward stand by what they have seen.

History tells us that during the war of 1812, the United States navy commissioned many privately owned ships to harass their bitter enemy, the British. One such vessel was the *Teazer*. She was caught and burned by the Brits in 1812. A gentleman's agreement was reached between the British and the *Teazer*'s officers: they would win their freedom if they promised not to engage in further attacks on British merchant ships. Naturally, the officers of the *Teazer*, including a Lieutenant Frederick Johnson, agreed. But promises are made to be broken, even by gentlemen. In time, the original *Teazer* was replaced by young *Teazer*, and who do you think proudly walked her deck? Lieutenant Frederick Johnson, himself, who had promised the British he would never again attack one of their ships. The day of reckoning came when young *Teazer* was being chased by two British warships. Rather than being caught and hanged, Lieutenant Johnson threw a flaming torch into the ship's powder magazine. In an instant, young Teazer reached skyward in a million pieces. The explosion was heard in the kitchens of Tancook and other islands in Mahone Bay.

It's been a long time since anyone has reported seeing this phantom of the sea. But she has been there, seen by fisherman who were so close to her that they said they could see men in her fiery riggings.

The Sea Ghost of Sable Island

This is one of my favorite Edith Mosher mysteries. It's from her book, *Haunted*.

It was in September 1856, when the American brigantine *Alma*, outward bound from New York and heading to St. John's, Newfoundland, was stranded about half a mile offshore on the treacherous shoals of Sable Island. A life-saving crew from the island station set off in a boat but ran into seas so heavy that the sturdy boat capsized before it could reach the stranded craft. The bow oarsman was thrown overboard and drowned. His body was never recovered.

On December 7 of that same year, another vessel, the schooner *Eliza Ross* from Sydney, got into trouble off Sable Island. The lifeboat crew, using the same lifeboat, again set out to attempt a rescue. As they rowed toward the distressed schooner, the men saw something that looked like the head of a man swimming. It was just about at the place where they had had the accident on their other mission. As they rowed closer they saw it was a man, but with eyes they had never before seen; vacant, staring eyes that seemed fixed on the distant horizon. Whatever it was seized the side of the boat and climbed aboard. Dripping, it sat on the vacant seat, grasped the oars and helped to row to the stranded vessel. This time the crew had better luck and were able to save the sailors on the doomed schooner. They pulled for shore, with the strange wild-eyed figure doing his share of rowing along with the others.

When they reached the place where he had boarded their boat, he dropped the oars, slid over the side, and vanished beneath the waves. The last thing the startled crew saw were the staring eyes as the waves swirled over the strange creature's head.

This ghost supposedly appeared several times to that same life-saving crew, but never attempted to enter the boat after a new man took the place of the drowned oarsman. Some said they had seen it, others denied that there was anything there to be seen. But all admitted to the feeling of their drowned friend in the boat with them.

A Fisherman's Shack

This story takes place in a fisherman's shack in a remote Nova Scotia village, where agonizing screams in the night kept all but the bravest behind locked doors. At one time, the shack in question, like so many others, was a warm and safe place for weary fishermen waiting for the out-going tide. But not any more; not since those terrible screams were indeed heard coming from inside the shack. The fishermen who went to investigate came away trembling and mumbling that the screams were coming from inside, but when they looked through the window, the place was empty!

Not long after the screams were first heard, a Cape Islander, not far offshore, floundered in a violent storm. Because of the raging seas, the local fishermen could only watch helplessly from the shore the sinking of the vessel. The villagers who stood on the banks could hear above the wind the screams of the fishermen aboard the sinking vessel. When the storm ended, the bodies of the fishermen who were washed up on shore were temporarily placed in a fisherman's shack—the same shack where the mysterious screams are heard. It was then the people of this remote fishing community understood the mystery surrounding those terrible screams. What they heard was a forerunner; a warning of an impending disaster, like that of the drowned fishermen who were washed up on their shores.

The fishing shack where this unholy story began is now gone. It is said a whale-oil lamp was thrown through a window late one night and burnt it to the ground. Still, some say that when they pass the spot where the shack once stood, they can still hear screams above the wind.

Chapter Four

Love and War

Millie's Last Ride

*I*t was a hot and dry Saturday afternoon when I stopped at a sidewalk cafe for something to quench my thirst. As I sat there sipping my drink, I noticed in the middle of the street the forming of a dust devil. Strange, I thought, very strange indeed, because there was on that unbearably hot afternoon absolutely no wind at all. But there it was beginning to take shape. Then it began to move snake-like toward me. Cars ran over it, but didn't crush it or break it into harmless tiny dust-devil pieces. I became hypnotized by it. It was upright, swaying its shapeless head from side to side as if searching out its prey. Then, what looked like one monstrous eye in the centre of this shapeless mass saw me and the dust devil bolted straight up. It moved slowly back and forth, gauging the distance, and then with lightening speed it came at me. But just before it reached me, it got caught up in a woman's skirt and disappeared.

As I finished my drink, the image of that dust devil took me back to a time I hadn't thought of since I was a child growing up in the Whitney Pier area of Sydney, where this story took place.

To avoid any embarrassment to the living, I refer to the couple in this story as only Millie and Rufus. Millie died on a cold December morning in 1912. She was eighty-five, and the last of her family. Millie, as everyone will agree, was a chronic complainer. She complained that her life was one of great hardship and suffering. What few friends she had thought otherwise. They believed she had it pretty good, considering she had become a widow twelve years earlier. That, they concluded, had to count for something. They should be so lucky.

Millie's bitterness was due to a failed relationship. She had been engaged to a young man who recognized something in Millie he didn't appreciate, so he disappeared for good.

Time being the great healer, she married Rufus, who eventually found out exactly what his new bride was like. Millie not only had a cruel streak, but also a vicious temper. If truth be known, on more than one occasion Rufus got the busy end of more than one air-born frying pan. Theirs was a marriage of convenience. For Millie, it kept food on the table; for Rufus, it meant having someone to cook the food. Needless to say, the relationship was soured from the beginning.

Rufus had but one true love in his life. Her name was Victoria—a green-eyed seventeen-year-old redhead, who died in a fire one cold winter's night. Rufus prayed for the day he would join his beloved in that other world.

One evening, after one beer too many in the local watering hole, Rufus boasted to his drinking buddies that he would get even with Millie. The day would come when he would make her pay. "We'll drink to that," his friends echoed, "but maybe in the next world, not in Millie's." Rufus smiled and thought to himself, yes, precisely, in the next world. Rufus then emptied his glass, said goodnight to his buddies and stepped out into the night. With unsteady legs he set off into the blackness. Halfway up Calvary Hill, Rufus was suddenly confronted by a brilliant blue light. There was no time to determine as to what was causing the illumination. Its force sent him to his knees and into the next world—and into the arms of his beloved, Victoria.

Twelve years had passed since Rufus died, and what he had feared the most while alive was about to happen. The woman who made his life on earth a living hell was about to lie down beside him for all eternity.

Moments before Millie died, she confessed that she may have been a little harsh with Rufus and prayed for his forgiveness. The old girl was hedging her bets. Millie did not fear death as much as she feared the unknown and Rufus's threats that he would get even with her from the next world. If he had the power, she would never get beyond the cemetery gates. Millie, now a frightened old woman, looked up at the familiar faces gathered around her bed and asked if that were possible? Could Rufus do that from the grave? With those fearful questions still on her lips, Millie gave a whimpering sigh and passed over. Outside, a wind came up and with it the worst snowstorm in memory.

On the morning of Millie's funeral, the snow had stopped, but lay deep throughout the region. With roads barely passable, it was wisely decided by the undertaker to transport Millie's body to the cemetery by horse and sleigh. What really concerned the undertaker was the old priest who was brought out of retirement on Millie's final wish, and the pallbearers, who were also all hand-picked by Millie herself. Most of them were well into their late seventies. It would be a miracle, the undertaker confided in his young assistant, if they didn't all drop dead before reaching the graveyard.

When the funeral mass ended, a small group of mourners came out of the church. Old men blew warm breath into their hands and stomped their feet to keep warm. The women stood some distance from the men and watched the six pallbearers struggling to keep Millie's coffin upright as they came down the church steps.

Millie's close friends wisely decided not to make the hazardous trek to the cemetery. They stood huddled against the icy wind and watched as the funeral procession made its way from out of the churchyard across the square and up Calvary Hill. Fighting to keep up were the old priest, his black robe dragging in the snow, and still further behind, the pallbearers.

Under hoof and under foot, there were three feet of snow. With fear in his heart the undertaker kept a tight rein on the horse as the animal lifted one heavy hoof after the other. Twice the animal stumbled and nearly fell. Fearing that the horse might indeed fall, the funeral director told his assistant to lead the animal by his head.

Halfway up the treacherous road, three of the pallbearers collapsed from exhaustion and spent the rest of the journey sitting on Millie's coffin.

When the procession reached the cemetery gates, a rumbling noise was heard. It appeared to be coming from just inside the graveyard, near a newly dug grave: Millie's grave. The awful noise sounded like high-pitched screaming. The old men covered their ears with their hands in an attempt to block out the terrible noise. Then they saw it! A black shape rising up out of the empty grave. The old priest fell to his knees blessing himself. Whatever it was, it spun into a cyclonic shape that grew bigger and bigger. Then it began spinning faster and faster until it became a shadowy white mass of snow, much like a prairie dust devil. It moved along the ground, under the gate, and slammed up against the horse. The startled animal, rearing up on its hind legs, fell over on its side, upsetting the sleigh. The three pallbearers who were sitting on Millie's coffin went sailing into the snowbank, while Millie and her coffin went careening back down the mountain. The undertaker and his assistant raced after the run-away coffin, but eventually gave up the chase. All they could do—anyone could do—was watch as the coffin disappeared down the mountain. What they didn't see, of course, was the coffin's disintegration when it slammed up against the railway abutment. Nor did they see Millie's body go sailing over the abutment. When her body came down on the other side, it landed on a moving train that was shunting a cargo of Cape Breton coal to waiting ships that were docked at the international coal piers. When the cars were positioned over the chute, the bottom doors of the car carrying Millie's body were opened and ten-thousand tons of coal, along with the body of Millie, went down into the ship's hold. The coal was destined for the furnaces of Upper Canada. Was the incident at the cemetery caused by the dead hand of Rufus? He did promise when alive to keep Millie from lying beside him for all eternity. Or was it merely a sudden burst of winter wind?

At the conclusion of a police investigation, the only evidence found were the broken pieces of the coffin. Millie's body was never recovered.

Weeks later, the old priest, still tormented by what he saw in the graveyard, went to see his Archbishop. "And what did you think you witnessed," asked the Archbishop.

"I saw the ghost of a young Rufus and a young woman. They were standing next to the newly dug grave. They just stood there watching."

"Excuse me, Father," said the Archbishop, "but you said you saw a young-looking Rufus. Rufus was over eighty when he died, wasn't he? How do you account for that?"

"I don't know," said the old priest, "but Rufus and I grew up together. I can't explain it, but it was Rufus I saw."

"And the young woman? Who was she?"

The old priest slowly raised his eyes to his superior and whispered, "Victoria!"

The Codfish Spook

*H*e is seen all over town, or so they tell us. You'd have to be blind to miss him, they say. He wears yellow oilskins and a sou'wester, and yes, he carries a codfish over his shoulder. He'll smile, step aside for the ladies, even tip his sou'wester, but he'll not give you the time of day, because he's not of our time any longer. Who is he? He's Saint John, New Brunswick's most colourful personality. One problem, though—he's a ghost! He's known around this old Loyalist town as the Codfish Spook.

So how did he end up in such an altered state? Well, from what we're told, love is what broke his heart, and water is what done him in—the waters of the Bay of Fundy to be exact. This isn't one of these Saint John brand of Irish folk-telling stories. No, according to most, this one's the real McCoy.

While on this earth, the spirit in question had a wife and five children. Keeping food on the table was more than a full time job. Old Codfish didn't mind, of course; he loved his wife and children.

Early one morning, while fishing for cod, he fell overboard and into the Bay of Fundy. One might imagine his last thought to have been, who is going to feed my wife and five little ones? Was it love and concern for his family that brought his spirit back from a watery grave?

There's some argument over where and when the Codfish Spook is seen around town. Some say only on the anniversary of his drowning; others contend, while coming out of a local watering hole on a Saturday night, that they see him all the time. When the fishing boats return to port, he's often seen coming up from the dock with a large cod slung over his shoulder. The Codfish Spook is heading home, where he'll leave the catch on his wife's doorstep, but not before looking inside to see the face of his beloved.

One morning, just before dropping off a fish, what he saw inside his former house set him back on his heels. There sitting at the head of the table was another sea-fairing lad! Well, even a spirit has feelings, and there were no longer any freebies! Not while there's another man "fishin' around!"

As the legend continues to unfolds, there are sightings of the Codfish Spook observing faces. Perhaps he's searching for a more appreciative soul. We have no proof, but have you noticed some of the more attractive Saint John widows hanging out in Market Square these days?

The Fortress Ghost

There are certain structures and places that convey a ghostly presence. On a dreary and fog-swept night, Fortress Louisbourg is such a place. In a house inside that great fortress, there is a strong presence other than human—I felt it as soon as I stepped over the threshold. The place in question was, and perhaps still is, the home of a Captain Robert Duhaget.

Ghosts usually keep to themselves, and for the most part move quietly in and out of their favourite haunts. When they accidentally confront the living, they're usually more upset that we are. But not in all cases. Not in the case of the ghost of Captain Robert Duhaget. He doesn't particularly care who sees him—and many employees of Fortress Louisbourg have.

Robert Duhaget was an officer of the Compagnies Franches de la Marine. He was no hero, nor did he distinguish himself in any great battle. Records show that he was slightly wounded during a mutiny by his own troops in Port Toulouse—now St. Peters, Cape Breton.

There are literally hundreds of documents chronicling the life and times of Fortress Louisbourg and its inhabitants. But nowhere is there a mention of any foul deed that may have kept this wandering soul from his grave. What the records do show, however, is that while returning to France, Duhaget died suddenly and was buried at sea. That may be why his spirit haunts the Fortress to this day.

The presence of the ghost was first felt by a worker who was in the attic of the Duhaget home. The employee remembers a man standing by the far wall of the attic wearing a red military greatcoat. At the time he thought the man was just another employee in costume sneaking a break. Both nodded to each other and the employee left. The second incident occurred while another staff member was seated in a chair by the fireplace. He was suddenly startled when a cold breeze swept past the right side of his face and then, as if it were an invisible person, crossed in front of him and then across his left cheek.

What really convinced the staff the home was haunted was when another employee, who was carrying boxes downstairs, stumbled and would have surely fallen if it hadn't been for someone, or something, from behind that grabbed her around the waist. The staff was convinced the ghost had to be Robert Duhaget.

The Duhaget spirit is also seen moving about the fortress grounds—passing sentries as he makes his way to the ramparts to inspect the guards on duty. And during evening prayers the spirit of Robert Duhaget enters the chapel. He sits by himself with his head bowed. Perhaps in some way he is praying to free his spirit and allow his wretched soul to return to France.

The Phantom Drummer

*W*hen he told them he heard the sound of a drum late one night coming from the direction of Fort Anne, they told him he must be hearing things. "No," he professed, "I didn't see anyone, but I did hear the sound of a drum and someone was playing "A Call to Arms.""

In 1605, middle class, upper class, lower class, priests and peasants alike, sailed from France to the new world, and were overwhelmed by what they saw when they sailed up the mouth of the Annapolis River. They exclaimed that "This is a place of wonder!" and they called it Annapolis Royal. In time, however, the British also wanted a piece of this paradise. Many battles ensued between these two powerful forces.

To protect their holdings, the British built Fort Anne. In 1710, and for the last time, the French were out and the British were in—in to stay. But nothing lasts forever; Annapolis Royal's political base would change. When Halifax was founded in 1749, Annapolis Royal was no longer the seat of power and the remaining soldiers at Fort Anne were shipped off to New Brunswick.

Today, Fort Anne is a portrait of what it was like back then. The old cemetery is a constant reminder of the sacrifices made by those early settlers. Resting under the hallowed ground of Fort Anne cemetery are hundreds of soldiers who are perhaps restless because they are unable to find peace in foreign soil. One such restless spirit may be the phantom drummer who is said to wander the ramparts playing "A Call to Arms."

No one has actually ever seen the phantom drummer, but the president of the Annapolis Royal society, Alan Melanson, has heard him. Alan's first encounter happened one evening, soon after he had retired for the night. For a moment he thought he was dreaming, but when he sat up in bed and listened, he knew someone was playing a drum. In the morning, he was told there was no emergency at the fort overnight. And no one was playing a drum.

Some tourists, we are told, while getting back on their buses, wonder where the soldier was—the one playing the drum.

Don't Walk Behind Me

*T*his story is from one of Edith Mosher's popular tales of the paranormal. I include it in her memory.

Ralph was a shy and quiet young farmer who rarely stopped long enough to pass the time of day with his neighbours. One day, Ralph arrived at the local general store and, following several attempts, told the owner that his wife, Martha, had left him for another man. When questioned about the other man, Ralph said he didn't know who he was. He was just guessing that's what she had done—run off and left him. Ralph's story surprised everyone and those who knew Martha could not believe she'd do such a thing. In time, however, no one was talking about Martha's disappearance—the whispering was about Ralph. His neighbours began noticing a drastic change in his behaviour. He started mumbling to himself and constantly looking over his shoulder as if someone was following him. Someone was—the ghost of Martha began dogging him. Poor Ralph never had a moment's peace. Even in death, there was no escaping her.

One afternoon, a farmer who was repairing his fence told his neighbours that he had watched Ralph coming down the road screaming over his shoulder, "Don't walk behind me!" All the farmer could see was Ralph. What he didn't see, of course, was Martha's ghost. Ralph now had a problem. He couldn't tell his family and neighbors what had actually happened to Martha. After all, he had to stick to his story that she had run off with another man. In the end, Ralph was committed to a psychiatric ward. Right there on the doctor's couch with the ghost of Martha watching, he ultimately confessed the whole sordid mess. He had murdered her because she was a busybody, a henpecking woman, he called her. He told the psychiatrist that Martha was appropriately enough, buried under the henhouse. Poor old Ralph was taken back to his room, babbling on, "The witch won't leave me alone. Ralph do this, Ralph do that, don't do that, Ralph."

When the police dug up what was left of Martha from under the henhouse and buried her in a proper grave, she no longer walked behind Ralph. It made little difference, though. In his present mental state, Ralph was in no condition to appreciate the end of Martha's henpecking.

The Ghost of Princess Lodge

*I*n 1794, Prince Edward, Duke of Kent, ordered his loyal subjects to build a domed music room for his mistress along the shores of Bedford Basin. This Halifax, Nova Scotia, landmark, known today as Princess Lodge, is the site of this tale of death and of a ghost that will not remain in his grave.

On a warm summer afternoon, Prince Edward invited a few of his friends on an afternoon of drinking and gambling. As the afternoon wore on, and the booze flowed freely, angry voices were heard over the calm waters of the basin. Two officers—an army colonel by the name of Ogilvie and a young naval lieutenant by the name of Howard—had become embroiled in a bitter dispute over the honour of a woman. Nothing short of a duel would satisfied either man.

It was dusk when both officers, with their seconds by their sides, faced each other. Then the stillness of the evening was broken by the clash of steel against steel. Colonel Ogilvie, a master swordsman in his own right, was no match for the quick and younger man. In a matter of minutes, Colonel Ogilvie fell to the ground, mortally wounded. The young naval officer was also wounded, but didn't die until days later.

It is not known where Prince Edward was at the time; perhaps he too fell—in this case from too much merriment. When he was told of the duel he became outraged. He reminded his officers that dueling was against military regulations. In his anger, the Prince ordered the body of Colonel Ogilvie buried where it had fallen, without military honours.

Not long after the burial, people began noticing a strange sight near the lodge. A lone figure later identified as Colonel Ogilvie could be seen rising up from his grave and wondering the grounds of Princess Lodge.

Legend has it that the ghost of Colonel Ogilvie will not rest until he's given a military burial. Until then, his spirit will continue to haunt the lodge. Some say if you look closely when day gives way to darkness, a lone figure in a red army tunic can be seen still wandering the royal grounds—waiting.

Chapter Five

Haunted
Holiday Spots

The Ghost of Haddon Hall

*T*here are people who believe that there is activity in the spirit world, and that spirits are, if you will, reluctant to give up the ghost. Spirits often come back, some never leave, because of a strong attachment to their home. If this is so, let this journey begin in a place where a ghost keeps a nightly vigil—a place where both humans and spirits cohabitate.

In the peaceful setting of Chester, Nova Scotia, sits an inn high on a hill overlooking Mahone Bay and its many islands.

Haddon Hall was built around the turn of the century and changed hands many times before it eventually fell into disrepair. It was rescued in 1993 and was restored to its former grace and beauty by its new owners.

Today, Haddon Hall is a warm, bright, and friendly place—visitors who stay the night agree, with one exception. When night falls, there is a dark side to Haddon Hall; there are peculiar sounds in the darkness, and for good reason, Haddon Hall, we are told, is haunted.

One morning while a maid was in the bathroom cleaning the tub, she was poked from behind. She knew she was alone in the room. When she told the other maids of her encounter with whatever it was, she was surprised to learn that they, too, had had similar experiences but each had kept it to herself. They all agreed that the place must be haunted and when they brought their suspicion to Cynthia O'Connell, the inn's manager. She merely smiled and told them, "yes, I know. I too have been contacted by the spirit." She told them to go about their work and not to be afraid; the ghost was a friendly spirit and means no harm.

Soon after, while one of the maids was making a bed, she felt the presence of a ghost in the room. Summing up all the courage she had, the maid turned around and said to the ghost, "I am here only to do my job and nothing else. Please leave me alone." From that moment on, she was never bothered again.

On another occasion, Cynthia O'Connel, who lived in an apartment in the back of the inn, awoke one night from a deep sleep to the sound of knocking on her bedroom door. When she went into the inn to investigate, thinking perhaps a guest had lost a key, there was no one at the door. When she returned to her apartment, she went into the living room to check on her pet dog, and her cockatoo bird. She found the bird lying on the cage floor nearly frozen to death. The portable heater she kept on to keep the bird warm had turned itself out and she was able to save the little bird just in time. To this day, no one can convince Cynthia that it wasn't the ghost who alerted her to the problem.

Another Chester resident who was a frequent visitor to Haddon Hall is Reverend Allan Gibson, now retired but knew the lady in question. There are skeptics of course, people who are hard to convince; but do keep an open mind. Reverend Gibson is convinced that the former owner of Haddon Hall, whom some believe is the ghost, was too nice a lady to actually scare anyone.

Ghosts, so we are informed, come in all shapes and sizes. After all, where they not like us at one time. Some have the power to appear or remain invisible. To be heard and understood or to remain silent. The Haddon Hall ghost makes her presence known in other ways.

On a personal note; when cameraman Jim Kevamman and I first arrived at Haddon Hall we were taken on a tour of the Inn and when we came out of this room we stood by the open door discussing the direction the story would take when suddenly the door slammed shut. We immediately opened the door and checked inside—no one was there. The windows were closed. The innkeeper's response, "Nothing unusual about that."

The Spirits of Grand Manan Island

Someone asked for the binoculars. Someone else said, "I don't believe it!" Another responded, "Oh my, oh my, you can believe it. That inn is haunted by ugly old women dragging behind them old men in chains!" Someone added, "And all through the night you can hear the dragging of chains over the floor and the moaning of the dead!" Another exclaimed, "I'm not staying there!"

We sailed past the rocky cliffs of New Brunswick's Grand Manan Island just as the fog was rolling over it. For better or worse, we were all registered at the inn that night. The inn is set back from the main road, and as you approach this gothic setting you feel as if you're being watched; it has a sinister and threatening look to it—an ill-feeling that's hard to shake off. And the place does have a questionable and shady past.

Someone explained: "Back in 1898, a Captain Jim Pettes sat down with a few of his cronies for a hand of poker. Either luck was on his side, or something was controlling the flow of cards his way. The old captain put down a royal flush in spades and left the card table with the deed to the inn—and maybe a curse on his new winnings from a poor loser!

Ol' Cap'n Pettes loved the inn, but not the location, so he had it moved next to the Marathon Inn. The new addition would be known as "The Annex."

Was there a curse put on the place? And who is haunting the Inn? From what we're told, and as you can read in Dorothy Dearborn's *Book of Ghosts and Demons*, three of the workmen involved in moving the inn were accidentally or mysteriously killed. According to the employees, at least one, or even all three of the dead workers haunt the inn. Those who have spent a sleepless night there tell of strange sounds in the room. One guest just up and left in the middle of the night because something was trying to chase her from her bed. Lamps were turned on and off, and even thrown across the room. When her securely locked door flew open, that did it. They found her in the morning at the ferry terminal asleep in her car. She couldn't wait to get off the island.

A short time later, a biologist from Pennsylvania retired for the night, and discerned a distinct whiff of lavender in the room. She kept still in her bed listening and waiting. Suddenly the bed began vibrating violently and the blankets flew across the room.

On another floor of the inn, a young husband and wife were kept awake all night while the taps in the sink and tub were being turned on and off.

Late one evening another guest, on her way back to her room, felt she was being followed. When she turned around, she saw the shape of what looked like a young man standing there watching her. Then he, or whatever it was, vanished.

The owner of the inn has yet to encounter the apparitions—at least that's the story he's sticking to. One thing he doesn't do is scoff at what guests tell him about their experiences with whatever it is that haunts the place.

When you leave Grand Manan and the Marathon Inn there is a feeling of relief. A feeling of escaping whatever it was that kept you awake.

The Ghost of Keltic Lodge

*E*ven a ghost is entitled to a holiday. And where else can you find a better setting than the famous Keltic Lodge in the highlands of Cape Breton? Some believe it's the rarefied air that brings back, time and time again, the spirit that haunts the lodge. Others say it's the isolation. The romantics believe it is love that keeps the spirit alive, or at the very least, active.

Not so long ago, a tourist who stayed at Keltic Lodge said she felt a strange feeling come over her the moment she stepped out of her car. Something she couldn't explain forced her to look up, and there in the window she saw a man staring down at her. The visitor said she couldn't shake the feeling the whole week she stayed at the lodge. One night when she was in the dining room with her husband and friends, she had to return to her room for something she had forgotten, and while hurrying down the long narrow corridor, that strange feeling grew much stronger. When she looked down the hall, there standing in the doorway was the same man she had seen when she first arrived. Needless to say, the lady did not go to her room; she turned on her heels and ran. When she told management about the stranger, she was informed that her description of the stranger did not fit any one on their staff, or for that matter any of the lodge's guests, but she was told the description did fit the original owner, who had died in the United States in the early 1930s. The lady exclaimed, "Then you have a non-paying guest! You have a ghost staying here!"

This is how this touching ghost story began and ended.

Deep and true love is forever. It crosses dimensions; it knows no boundaries. The ghost in this story fell in love with another ghost! It is a tender tale from the highlands.

In the late nineteenth century, Henry Corson of Ohio was told by the family doctor that his wife was suffering from tuberculosis. If she was to survive, she must move out of the city to the country, where there was plenty of clean, fresh air. Accordingly, young Mr. Corson took his wife on a long and leisurely holiday that included a visit with their friend Alexander Graham Bell, who lived in Baddeck, Nova Scotia. Mr. Bell took the Corsons on a trip over Cape Smokey. Once they arrived at the top of the highlands, and took in the breathtaking view, the Corsons noticed a point of land jutting out into the ocean and they immediately knew they had found their paradise.

At that time, a large log home was built near where Keltic Lodge now stands. The Corson estate soon became famous for its trees and orchards. Young Mr. Corson was also an astute businessman; he raised cattle and owned and operated a thriving dairy farm. But nothing lasts forever. Apparently the Highlands did agree with Mrs. Corson, who was not only cured of her illness, but outlived her husband. Loneliness and the pressures of business, however, forced the widow to return permanently to her home in Akron, Ohio. Just as well, because in the mid-1930s, the strong arm of the government reached and expropriated Corson's property to create parklands. Local legend maintains that when Mrs. Corson died, her spirit came back to her beloved highlands to be with the spirit of her husband. Some ask why only the ghost of old Henry haunts the lodge. Perhaps he's still looking after his investments, and then again, maybe he's angry over the government's land grab!

The Ghost of Oscar Wilde

"*I*f someone is there, show yourself. Please don't scare me so!" That's what the lady from Massachusetts told the desk clerk she had said to the strange figure who'd appeared in her room the night before she checked out.

"Did you actually see anyone?" asked the clerk.

"Of course I did. He was tall. Wore a wide-brimmed hat and a cape over his shoulders and he was reading from a book he had in his hand. His lips were moving, but I couldn't hear him."

"Oh, him," said the clerk, "that was Oscar."

"Oscar? Oscar who?" asked the lady.

"Oscar Wilde—I mean the ghost of Oscar Wilde."

That incident supposedly happened sometime in the mid-1980s. And there have been many similar reports since then.

It was a hundred years earlier when poet and dramatist Oscar Wilde first arrived on our shores. Halifax and Saint John were the first two cities scheduled on his North American tour. And yes, while in Halifax, Mr. Wilde did indeed stay at the Waverley Inn on Barrington Street. For a hefty fee, Mr. Wilde would visit your home and entertain you and your friends by reading from his poetry.

Oscar must have been quite a sight to see walking down Barrington Street. He was one of the most outrageous dresser of the Victorian age, often wearing green velvet pantaloons and gold buckle shoes.

Following his whirlwind visit to Halifax, Oscar promised his new friends that he loved the city and its people so much, that he would return one day. That promise was never kept—or was it?

Some companies will go to any lengths to promote their business interests. However, the staff and management of the Waverley Inn have never actually said they've the ghost of Oscar Wilde in residence.

In all fairness, it's the weary traveller who says the inn is haunted. But the descriptions they give of the ghost fit Oscar right down to his pantaloons.

There is, in his honour, an Oscar Wilde room at the Waverley. Should your sleep be interrupted by this lively spirit, fear not—he's probably just looking for an audience; he loves to hear his own voice reading from one of his own works.

The Moxham Castle Ghost

It was after midnight when I checked in at Sydney's Holiday Inn. Next morning at breakfast, the waitress greeted me with a smile, a much welcomed cup of coffee and a question. Actually, it was more of a statement than a question: "You know, Mr. Jessome, we have a ghost right here in the inn." Hmmm, I thought. So, while I sipped my coffee, she told me the story of the mysterious ghost. Being a romantic, the waitress believed the motel was haunted because the ghost had supposedly stayed here for part of her honeymoon. She added; "And who knows, maybe the husband died or was killed and when the wife died, her spirit returned to the place where they had been happy young lovers." As an after thought, she said, "Then again, maybe there's a connection with Moxham Castle." The castle had once stood on the site of the Holiday Inn. That observation sparked my interest, so I agreed to investigate.

According to the housekeepers and waitresses I interviewed at the Holiday Inn, the ghost in residence wanders aimlessly in the long and narrow corridors of the lower level of the inn. She has also been seen passing straight through the walls and doors into rooms.

One housekeeper in particular was singled out by the ghost. Debbie Macdonald remembered encountering the spirit while doing housekeeping duties on the lower level. Debbie said she felt a strong presence when she came out of a room to get clean linen from her cart. Although she couldn't see anyone, she was certain that whomever, or whatever, it was, was standing there watching her. Debbie tried to shake the feeling, but it became much stronger. In the end, she gathered up enough courage to confront the spirit. "Please tell me what is it you want and who you are. Tell me, or leave me alone!" Debbie Macdonald was never bothered again. However, she did leave the Holiday Inn for a similar job at another motel.

Remembering the waitress' comment about a possible connection between the ghost and Moxham Castle, I looked for a possible connection and found one!

At the Holiday Inn, speculation about the ghost is rampant. "Could it be the ghost in question is the lady of Moxham Castle, Mr Jessome?"

"Don't know."

"Maybe, Mr. Jessome, her spirit is haunting the motel because she missed the castle so much that when she died, her spirit came back and finding the castle gone, she is forever lost in the Holiday Inn?" Who really knows.

I said my goodbyes and checked out. On the drive to the airport I wondered who the ghost really was. The next time you visit my fair city and you need lodgings for the night, the Holiday Inn may offer you something more than a good night's sleep.

The Dueling Ghosts

*T*he Royal Bank of Canada in Annapolis Royal was built on the property where an inn once stood. It was a popular inn especially for travellers and the military. The inn was constructed in the early 1800s and before it was torn down, was the domain of not one, but two lively military spirits.

This is what a young army officer who stayed overnight at the inn told his fiancée the following day: No sooner was he comfortably in bed when he heard something strange outside his door. It was as if something or someone was trying to push through the door, which was bolted from the inside—whomever it was would have to smash it down to get in. Even so, he was afraid. Suddenly, the door burst open and two ghost-like figures wearing the uniforms of officers began dueling. The young man sat there transfixed, listening to their heavy breathing and the crashing of steel against steel. The duel went on all night until one of the officers plunged his sword into the chest of the other. The young man watched in horror as the officer severed the hand of the dead soldier—the hand that held the sword. He then lifted the body and hurled it through the open window to the courtyard below.

There is a further connection between the inn and the bank. In 1870, when the foundation was being dug for the bank—known then as the union bank of Halifax—the skeletal remains of an army officer were uncovered. Was it the body of the officer who was thrown out the window of the inn? Some say the right hand of the skeleton was missing! A coincidence?

Nelson's Ghost

*T*his Maritime Mystery comes from Pleasant Point, Nova Scotia. It's a peaceful place where the waters of Musquodoboit Harbour wash up on its shore—so pleasant a place that the ghost of Admiral Horatio Nelson decided this was where he'd find companionship and eternal rest.

Ivan and Mildred Kent, who operate a bed and breakfast in Pleasant Point, knew they had a ghost living in their lighthouse, but didn't know for a long time who it was.

Ivan claims there's a family connection between his family and Admiral Nelson. Ivan's great-grandfather, William Thomas Kent, was born in England, and joined Nelson's flagship as a navigator. He was aboard the *Victory* when Nelson was mortally wounded in the battle of Trafalgar, and escorted the admiral's body back to England.

Following a distinguished career in the British navy, Lieutenant Kent immigrated to Canada and was, until his retirement, governor of Melville Island Prison in Halifax. Kent then moved his family to a home he built at Pleasant Point.

In the early 1900s, the old homestead was torn down and a lighthouse was built on the site. End of Nelson's ghost? No, it simply moved into the lighthouse. But Ivan and his wife Mildred didn't know who the ghost was until a psychic visited the area. While exploring the grounds one day, the psychic's visit to the lighthouse was cut short. No sooner was she about to climb the steps to the top, when she quickly left, telling her companion that the place was haunted. Sometime later, the Kents received a letter from the psychic telling them that the ghost was none other than Admiral Horatio Nelson. That letter awakened in Ivan the exploits of his great-grandfather, and his connection with Admiral Nelson.

Ivan, with his back to the famous lighthouse, paused and smiled as he remembered the story that was handed down from one generation of Kents to the next: "When Nelson's spirit returned to Portsmouth, it realized his body was going to be taken up to London for a hero's burial. "What the hell was the point of me going up there with that miserable body of mine? It only had one eye and one arm anyway. Instead, I'll join my navigator friend, William Kent, who's still a young man with a lot of sailing left in him. And that's what the ghost of Nelson did until his shipmate retired and immigrated to Nova Scotia."

Ivan Kent respects what comes over from the spirit world; he wants to keep them happy. He reminds tourists that the picnic table he placed near the lighthouse is reserved for his two permanent guests from 10 P.M. until 4 A.M: a place where they can reminisce about the glory days at sea.

Should you not heed the warning and sit down at the picnic table, you may feel something or someone pushing you off…

Mehetible's Ghost

St. Andrews-by-the-Sea has an old world charm and warmth about it, but is full of ghosts of the past. Walk any of its streets when day slips into darkness and the night brings long-forgotten sounds: the rustling of a woman's skirt, the sounds of horse and carriage rolling over cobblestones. As you make your way down Water Street, you can feel a strong presence of those who first settled this New Brunswick town more than two hundred years ago.

Natives fished the Passamaquoddy long before anyone else, then the Irish came, followed by the Empire loyalists. Among the Loyalist families that fled the American Revolution were the Mowatts and the Caleffs. Young Captain David Mowatt would eventually marry Doctor Caleff's daughter, Mehetible. Very little has changed in this quaint seaside town since Mehetible's time.

Old landmarks are still visible and most of the homes and businesses along Water Street still stand, as does Windsor House, the home Captain Mowatt built for Mehetible In 1798.

Today Windsor house, now an inn, has a new lease on life, brought back to its glory days by Jay Remer and Greg Cohane.

Those who were involved in the restoration of Windsor House were aware of a strong presence and everyone agreed that it was the ghost of Mehetible Califf Mowatt. Mehetible outlived her husband, who died at sea. She continued living in the home well into her 90s and was, in the end, the last Empire Loyalist living in St. Andrews. Her spirit is felt most often late at night and early in the morning—that's when footsteps are heard and things get re-arranged.

If you visit or stay overnight in Windsor House, you'll notice a marvellous collection of water colours by New Brunswick artist Anthony Flowers, who lived during Mehetible's time. There is a wall that leads upstairs where Flower's paintings hang, and every morning they have to be straightened.

While visiting Windsor House, I asked which bedroom had been Mehetible's. I was directed to the one at the top of the stairs; the one they have to unlock every morning. Spend time alone in that room and you'll feel an energy, and the sensation you're been watched.

Next time you visit New Brunswick, and you're close to St. Andrews, visit Windsor House Inn. And, if you stay overnight, remember Mehetible's bedroom is at the top of the stairs—the one on the left. Pleasant dreams.

The Strathgartney Ghost

"She was a mysterious and unfortunate young woman, Gracie Grey was." That's how the old folk put it when they talked about poor, frozen, Gracie Grey.

Gracie grew up in Bonshaw, Prince Edward Island, in the 1850s. She lived in the grand country estate of Robert Bruce Stewart. Stewart was born in England in 1813 and in 1846, he, his wife, and their five children set sail for Prince Edward Island. They arrived in Charlottetown in the fall of the same year. In time, Robert Bruce Stewart would become one of the Island's most notorious land barons.

He settled in Bonshaw, some twenty miles outside of Charlottetown. This home was built on one of the highest hills on the Island and had an excellent view of the Northumberland Strait. Proud of his Scottish heritage, Stewart named his estate Strathgartney, after the place where his father had been born. Today, Strathgartney is a popular inn. Robert Bruce Stewart's clan eventually included nine children and perhaps, unofficially, one other; Gracie Grey.

Some Islanders will tell you that the spirit of Gracie Grey still haunts the hollows and hills of Bonshaw. No one of such a tender age as Gracie is expected to die, and least of all become a ghost, but that's exactly what happened to Gracie.

It was a cold winter's afternoon in 1888 when death claimed Gracie. She had set off for the village to buy some needed staples for the Stewart's table. On her return, she was caught in a sudden and violent snow storm, so bad, it would be known as the great blizzard of 1888. No one in the Stewart household was concerned when she didn't return to Strathgartney. The Stewarts knew Gracie would find shelter in a neighbour's home. But that was not to be. Just yards from the warmth and safety of Strathgartney, Gracie, struggling against the punishing storm, collapsed. Her cries for help were lost in the howling wind.

Three days later, searchers came upon the basket Gracie had hung on a tree branch. Buried deep in the snow below was the frozen body of young Gracie Grey. The searchers carried her frozen body inside Strathgartney to her bedroom on the third floor.

It was not long after her death that strange things began happening. Her ghost first appeared roaming the grounds, or standing down by the gate where she had died. Other times people reported seeing her ghost walking along the road. The former premier of the province, Walter Shaw, wrote in his book, *Tell me the Tales*, that his father's and Gracie Grey's paths crossed on St. Catherine's Road near a place known as Gloomy Blues Hollow. When he told his friend this, he was warned to watch out for the ghost of Gracie Grey.

Most of the time, though, her spirit remained on the third floor of Strathgartney wandering in and out of her bedroom. A weaver's loom that Gracie operated would often start weaving by itself; a sure sign that Gracie was in the room.

The most frightening incident, however, occurred when Gracie's brother was riding home over the same road that Gracie had travelled the day she died. Her brother felt something pulling on the right stirrup of his saddle. When he looked down, there was his sister, or the ghost of his sister, walking alongside the horse.

When he arrived at Strathgartney, he collapsed and was under doctor's care for many weeks.

Today, those who know their Bonshaw history, will tell you that when you're inside Strathgartney Inn, or walking down by Gloomy Blues Hollow, you are not alone!

The Ghost of Jenkins House

New Brunswick has a rich, diverse history full of bountiful folklore. A mere mention of the Miramichi, for example, and up pop tales of the ghosts of the headless nun, and of the Dungarven Whooper.

For this gem of the paranormal, we return to the year 1810 in the village of Gagetown, where a Scotsman by the name of Hugh Johnson built a two-and-a-half storey mansion. It became, with its four chimneys, quite a head-turner. In later years, this stately mansion became the residence of the world-renowned weaver and tartan designer, the late Patricia Jenkins. The home is still in the Jenkins family and it is now known by that name. The mansion stands as a reminder that if there was joy in the home, it was also a place of tragedy. The eldest daughter of Hugh Johnson died there in childbirth. And one of his sons and his fiancée were killed when their carriage overturned.

During the last century, several people who lived in Jenkins' house have reported seeing the ghost of a woman moving from room to room. She is, according to those who have lived under that roof, not a mean spirit; she's more benevolent than anything else. There have been times, however, when she has sent a certain picture crashing to the floor. Why? No one knows. Some theorize it was an attention-getter or that she simply didn't like it!

While visiting relatives who owned the home at the time, a young girl retiring for the night sat straight up in bed when a woman came out of the closet and walked past her to the window. The girl described the woman as wearing a white dress and having shoulder-length hair. Thinking it was her aunt, she asked, "What's wrong?" The woman neither turned around or spoke. She simply vanished!

Years later, while attending a family member's wake, that same girl, now an adult, listened to her uncle tell the story of a young woman from Saint John who, along with her younger sister, travelled to Gagetown, where the woman's engagement to Hugh Johnson's son was to be officially announced. But the young man took one look at his fiancée's younger sister and fell deeply in love with her instead. Needless to say, the marriage was off.

Sometime after that, and feeling sorry or guilty, the couple invited the jilted sister-in-law to come live with them. Unable to accept, or bear seeing her younger sister in the arms of the man she still loved, the woman got a rope went upstairs and hanged herself in the closet of her bedroom. The young woman listening to her uncle's story remembered her own experience as a young child and even before she asked her uncle which bedroom, she knew what the answer would be. But the elderly uncle wasn't through telling about that old house and what he had seen there. One night, he told his frightened and captive audience, while in bed in that very same room, he saw a woman in white walk into the closet. Thinking it was one of the women looking for some clothes, he waited, but she never came out.

For most people who lived in the Jenkins Home, including Patricia Jenkins, all they've ever heard were odd sounds such as the rustling of skirts going by. But all agree there is a spirit there.

Chapter Six

Possessions
and Church Tales

The Spook Farm

*T*his story was first brought to my attention by my late camera man, Kevin Macdonald. Later, when I began researching this bizarre story, people in the know suggested that I should pick up a copy of N. Carroll Macintyre's *The Fire-Spook of Caledonia Mills*— an excellent account of this odd story, they told me. So, I give credit to both of these talented people.

The journey begins in a place called Caledonia Mills.

Caledonia Mills is nothing to write home about, unless you like a quiet rural setting. It's what happened there seventy-five years ago that had many people writing home about the place and its strange occurrences.

Without drawing you a map, Caledonia Mills is a small farming community some fifteen miles from the town of Antigonish, Nova Scotia.

The curious will be disappointed if they expect to find the homestead in this tale still standing. The house and barns are long gone. There was a time, though, back in the early twenties, when it was the home of Alexander "Black John" MacDonald, his wife Janet, and their adopted daughter, Mary Ellen. An older daughter, also named Mary, married William Quirk and moved off the farm to Alder River, N.S.

There were peculiar and unexplained things happening in the MacDonald household that the family kept secret for several years. It began when neighbours found belongings of the MacDonald household strewn near their property. The answer given by the MacDonalds?—blame it on the dog. No one bought that story when they later found pots and large cast iron skillets all over the place. No dog could do that.

Things became a lot more serious the day that Alex found the animals in the barn loose from their stalls when he went to feed and water them in the morning. He knew he had secured them the night before. The bizarre things that were happening were a harbinger of things to come.

One morning in the winter of 1922, while Alex was starting a fire in the kitchen stove, he noticed burnt pieces of wood on top of the stove. When he checked for the source, he saw charred areas in the rafters just above the stove. When the family retired that night, Janet MacDonald was awakened by the smell of smoke. Alex raced downstairs and found a chair and sofa on fire in the kitchen. All told, there were thirty-eight fires in the month of January alone! No longer able to cope alone, the family were forced to call in the neighbours for help. A few of the men of the village did help in fighting these mysterious fires. One witness said it was as if the whole house was illuminated by the blue arc of a hot electrical cable during a violent storm. It was a losing battle. Whatever power it was, the MacDonalds were driven from their home. They did attempt to return, but once again the demons had taken over, and drove them out.

What caused these fires? A poltergeist perhaps? There were several theories advanced. One: Janet MacDonald had taken her mother from the poor house and brought her to live with them at the farm. In time, Janet realized that she had made a terrible mistake—her mother was an uncontrollable raving mad woman. When she attempted to send her back, the authorities told her it was Janet's problem now. One day, a visitor was witness to one of the old lady's ravings and saw Janet race upstairs to her mother's bedroom screaming, "I hope the Devil comes and takes you before nine o'clock tomorrow morning!" Just then, a strange looking black animal came into the old woman's bedroom.

There would be no more screams, no more fits of rage. The next morning, Alexander found Janet's mother dead in bed. Official cause of death was never mentioned. Did she die under mysterious circumstances? By suffocation perhaps? By someone else's hand? But whose?

Surely, calling on the Devil to take someone is merely wishful thinking. Or is it? And was that strange looking animal, thought to be a dog, dismissed out of hand? Did the spirit of that crazed old woman return to reek vengeance on the MacDonald household?

The professionals:

Peter Owen "peachy" Carroll, a one-time police chief of the town of Pictou and a member of the provincial detective force of Nova Scotia, became intrigued by what was happening at the Spook Farm and made arrangement to investigate. Detective Carroll was quite confident that he would solve this Maritime Mystery.

Accompanying Mr. Carroll was Halifax Herald reporter, Harold Whidden, who would have an important role to play in this drama.

Alexander "Black John" MacDonald agreed to open his home to Carroll and Whidden, and also agreed to stay in the house with them.

Detective Carroll made a thorough investigation of the interior of the home. He saw the scorched walls, wallpaper, and blinds. He interviewed the MacDonald family and concluded they were God-fearing hard-working folk, and had no hand in setting the fires.

The only unusual occurrence happened on the second night. When Carroll and Whidden had retired while still awake, Whidden was slapped across the arm. Carroll denied hitting him.

After reviewing all the "facts," Carroll concluded, that the fires were not started by human hands, but by an unknown force.

Carroll and Whidden went so far as to offer a reward of $200 to anyone who could prove the fires were caused by any agent other than the supernatural.

The news of the fire spook reached far beyond the counties of Antigonish and Guysborough. Interest was shown from all over North America and beyond. From the city of New York, a Dr. Walter Franklin Prince, a member of the American Society for Psychical Research who displayed more than a passing interest, was willing to come to Nova Scotia and investigate this phenomenon. But for a price.

His expenses would be underwritten by the *Halifax Herald*.

If there were any spirits attempting to make contact with the living, Dr. Prince believed he had the conduit in the person of Harold Whidden, who, again, went along, with other observers, as the *Herald*'s representative. Mr. Whidden was more than familiar with the Spook Farm, having already spent two days and nights there with Peachy Carroll. Dr. Prince believed Harold Whidden would be a receptive candidate for psychological testing. When Dr. Prince finally got around to doing the test, he sat Whidden down at a table with pencils and paper and instructed him to hold the pencil above the paper and see what happened. The first three attempts failed, but on the fourth try, Whidden felt a sensation in his fingers and the pencil in his hand flew across the page. Not just one page, but several. Dr. Prince then conducted an interview with the spirit.

Question: Who set the fires in the Alexander MacDonald home?

Answer: Immediately written down on paper through Whidden's hand, the word "Spirits!"

Question: Why?

No answer. The pencil was taping quickly on paper, but only black marks were made.

And then, a voice spoke through Whidden. It told the people in the room to leave. Only Dr. Prince was to remain!

Question: Did you slap the arm of Mr. Whidden when he and Detective Carroll were staying here?

Answer: The word "Yes" was immediately written down.

Question: Why?

Answer: Again, Whidden's hand flew across the page. "I wanted him to know the fires were caused by spirits."

Question: And the animals in the barn? Who let them loose?

Answer: "I did."

The spirit also wrote that it would no longer haunt the MacDonalds, nor would it ever appear to them again, just as long as they did not return to the farm.

There were many more questions and answers. The spirit, through the hand of Harold Whidden, gave the reason for setting the fires, and gave its name! What followed, according to Dr. Prince, was of a personal and delicate nature. Because of that, the highly sensitive information revealed by the spirit was never released.

But witnesses confirmed the story of what happened in the room that night.

Following a six-day investigation, Dr. Prince concluded that the fires were started by the adopted daughter, Mary Ellen. Dr. Prince said no blame should be placed on Mary Ellen because she was in a state of altered consciousness at the time; she had been temporarily possessed.

MacIntyre writes in the final chapter of his book,

"This is the part of the strange manuscript of automatic writing by Harold Whidden, which was never released for public knowledge: Whidden of course knew, Dr. Walter Prince knew, others present knew, as did a priest from St Andrew's, but their lips were sealed. It has only been in the past few months that certain people who knew the true story would confide in me enough to hint as to the deep, dark secret that has been kept so well buried for the past sixty-three years. They knew that Mary Ellen was innocent as to the cause of the strange occurrences, even though they may have acted through her. They knew it was upon the head of Janet "Black John" where the blame should be placed; blame that had kept people guessing for all those years.

Did the MacDonalds heed the warning of the spirit never to return to the farm? They did not. In time, and because they missed their home, they did return. For a little while things appeared normal. So much so that Alex "Black John" decided to plant a spring crop. But a black cloud hung over the MacDonald farm. In less than three weeks, the fires started again. The MacDonalds fought these demons secretly, but in the end were forced to give up and leave the Spook Farm for good.

And what eventually happened to the principal players in this Maritime Mystery?

Alexander "Black John" MacDonald died on March 26, 1923, of natural causes at the home of his daughter, Mary Quirk.

Mary Ellen "Black John" MacDonald stayed in the area for a year and then moved to Ontario where she operated a boarding house. When she died, her remains were brought back to Nova Scotia for burial.

Janet "Black John" MacDonald died on March 17, 1930, also at the home of her daughter, at the age of eighty. Cause of death—third degree burns!!!

So the journey ends ... or does it?

One final warning: If you should go down Caledonia Mills way and you're trudging through the woods and accidentally come upon a clearing where there should be ample growth of trees and flowers and singing birds, but instead you find barren ground, then you have stumbled onto the property of Alexander "Black John" MacDonald. That barren piece of land you're standing on is the spot where the Spook Farm once stood. Nothing grows there anymore! And if you take a souvenir, such as a charred and broken piece of shingle, you do so at your own peril. Take it home and who knows where the next mysterious fires may start! The author of *The Fire-Spook of Caledonia Mills* took an egg cup from the charred ruins. He of all people should have known better. Mr. MacIntyre placed the egg cup on the fireplace mantel of his summer home one holiday weekend and left. The only thing left standing in the morning was the chimney!

There are, even today, people living in Caledonia Mills who will not drive by the Spook Farm late at night, for fear of having a breakdown, mechanical or mental!

The Holy Ghost

The events I'm about to describe are from the pen, or rather the tongue of another, as it's an oral account. He, and he alone, is the author of this adventure into the paranormal. My only purpose is to continue the gifted tradition of that dying breed—the storyteller.

This spiritual tale came to my attention by way of Mickey MacNeil's story about a Priest who was owed a mass. This delightful piece of folklore, along with other delights, can be found in Ronald Caplan's *Cape Breton Book of the Night.*

Although I may have taking some liberties in the telling of this island yarn, the facts have not been altered one iota. This is how the tale unfolds:

Sometime around the turn of the century in a rural community in Cape Breton, a young boy was accused of stealing money from the church poor box. Discipline was harsh in those days, and the child would pay dearly for this alleged crime. The parish priest would teach this young scoundrel a lesson he would remember for the rest of his life. His punishment? Three nights locked up alone in the church. Apparently, no one thought the punishment unreasonable. The boy was taken from his home at the appointed hour and handed over to the priest, who locked the frightened child inside the church. The boy was left alone to consider his crime.

The church, like the graveyard that surrounded it, was wrapped in deadly silence. The only light was a thin sliver that squeezed through a crack in one of the stained glass windows. Its beam fell on the head of the child. As he struggled to fend off sleep, the church was suddenly illuminated with a radiant yellowish hue, and filled with the scent of flowers. The boy's eye caught a movement on the altar. It was like mist coming up from somewhere below. Transfixed, he watched it take on a human shape; the shape of an old priest. Scared out of his wits, the boy remained motionless, hoping against all hope that he wouldn't been seen by the strange-looking priest. With outstretched arms, the priest, with great sorrow and in a mournful voice, cried out, "Who will assist me in the mass?" Too frightened to speak, the boy shut his eyes and prayed that whatever it was would disappear. Again, the voice of the priest cried out, "Help me, help me!" When the boy summoned enough courage to look up, the old priest was gone.

In the morning, the boy was sent home, but he told no one of what he had seen. Would anyone really believe him? The next night the boy was locked inside the church again. At midnight the church once more came alive with a brilliant light. And out of a mist appeared the old priest who raised his arms and in a wailing voice again asked, "Who will assist me in the mass?" The boy remained quiet, still too afraid to make his presence known.

On the third night, the young boy moved closer to the altar and waited. At exactly midnight, the old priest appeared, and when he asked if there was anyone who would assist him, the boy with his heart pounding in his chest stood up and said, "I will assist you, Father."

When the mass was over, the ghost told the boy that he had died on the altar while saying the mass over fifty years ago and he could not rest in his grave until he completed the mass. He explained that now, thanks to the boy his soul could find eternal rest.

In the morning the parish priest reminded the young boy of what he had done and said he hoped that he had learned a valuable lesson while locked inside the church. The child looked up at the priest and said, "Yes, I learned a lot, and you know something, Father, I did something that I don't believe you'll ever do."

"And what is that?" asked the priest.

The boy smiled and said, "I helped an old priest get to heaven last night."

The Headless Nun

$\mathcal{I}$t was late, and darkness had swept over the Miramichi, making the way treacherous for the old man who was moving slowly toward the bridge that crossed over Crow Brook. Not only was he fighting a cold winter's wind, but inside him was the fear of having been confronted by the ghost of the Headless Nun. He trudges on.

The story of the Headless Nun is perhaps the most famous of all the ghost stories to come out of the Miramichi.

Two New Brunswick writers, Harold W. J. Adams and writer/teacher Doug Underhill, wrote extensively on this piece of history and folklore.

The tale of the Headless Nun got its beginnings during the 1700s in the French Fort Cove region of New Brunswick. When the Acadians were driven out of Nova Scotia in 1756, many made their way to Louisiana and Quebec, while others stopped in northern New Brunswick, where they set up a small community not far from what is now known as New Castle. It was Harold Adams who gave the ghost the name Sister Marie Inconnus, meaning the "unknown one."

Of major concern to the community during this period was the constant threat that the British would eventually overrun French Fort Cove and not only kill or drive off the inhabitants, but also confiscate their valuables. To prevent this, the community placed all their money, jewellery, and gold in a large treasure chest. Sister Marie was trusted with the safety of the treasure and it was she who selected the place where the treasure was buried. The news of buried treasure and who knew where it was hidden spread throughout the Miramichi. One day while crossing the Crow Brook Bridge, Sister Marie was brutally attacked by a woodsman, who, when she wouldn't tell him where the treasure was buried, cut off her head and ran into the woods with it. Another version has two men attacking her on the same bridge and when she refused to tell them where she hid the treasure, one of the robbers severed her head. When they realized what they had done, they threw the head into the water below and fled.

The body of Sister Marie was found the next morning by French soldiers. However, a search party that combed the river and woods never did find the severed head of Sister Marie Inconnus. In time, the body was returned to France.

Not long after that gruesome murder, the ghost of Sister Marie was seen walking back and forth over the Crow Brook Bridge, searching for her missing head.

The old man approaching the bridge stopped. His old eyes peered into the darkness. The only sound was the wind and rushing waters below. He took a deep breath and stepped onto the bridge. Near the other side, a black form appeared out of nowhere. Above the wind, he heard a whispering cry, "Please help me find my head so that I can become whole again." The old man collapsed. When he came to, the ghost of the headless Nun had vanished.

Most of French Fort Cove, as it was then, is gone. Still popular is the theory that there was treasure buried in or around the old French Fort Cove region. And on cold winter nights, the ghost of the headless Nun crosses the Crow Brook Bridge.

The Great Amherst Mystery

If there is one story dealing with the paranormal that has left a lasting impression on me, it's the extraordinary and frightening account of a young woman who became possessed by demons. Locals go in and out of the Canadian Tire store on Princess Street in

Amherst, Nova Scotia, by the hundreds, unaware of the terrible events that happened at that location 120 years ago. But those who know the tale, are filled with an uneasy foreboding.

In 1878, there was a row of small homes on Princess Street. In one such modest dwelling lived eighteen-year-old Esther Cox, who would in time become the centre of this unbelievable drama. Esther's mother had died when she was an infant, and her father had remarried and moved to the United States. No one knows why he abandoned his children.

Esther and her sister moved in with their aunt and uncle, Daniel and Olive Teed. It was a happy and tight-knit family, until one evening when Esther and her sister had retired for the night. Esther became restless. She tossed and turned and complained that something was happening to her; something inside her body that she didn't understand. Her sister scolded her, telling her that people would think she was crazy and if she kept it up, she'd be carried off to an insane asylum. That night, Esther cried herself to sleep.

For this young Amherst, Nova Scotia, woman, what happened that night was just the beginning of a terror-stricken trip into the world of demons. A poltergeist was now in residence in the Teed home and in the body of one Esther Cox.

Nothing much out of the ordinary happened for about a week. Then one night while Esther and her sister had retired for the night, something awakened Esther. She felt something moving in the bed. She stiffened and jumping out of bed, and screamed that there were mice crawling under the sheets! When her sister tore the bedclothes back, the bed was empty. Then, to their horror, they saw something moving under the bed. It was a box containing patchwork. They stood there stupefied as the box slid across the floor to the middle of the room, where it lifted off the floor as if by some unknown force, and then fell back down again. When the Cox sisters called their uncle, he checked the box and, finding nothing unusual, told his nieces to go back to bed and then left the room laughing.

Near dawn, Esther jumped out of bed again screaming, "I'm dying, I'm dying!" Esther's screams awakened the whole family, who rushed to her bedroom. There they found Esther with her hair standing on end and her skin turning the colour of blood. When the family finally calmed her down and got her back in bed, what they witnessed next nearly drove them from the room. Esther's body began swelling to an enormous size. Suddenly there was a mysterious explosion of noise, so powerful that it shook the entire house. When the noise stopped, Esther's body returned to its normal size.

Life for Esther Cox would only get worse. On subsequent nights, bedclothes were ripped off her bed and objects went flying across the room.

One evening, when Esther's health was at its lowest ebb, a doctor was summoned. During the examination, and with the family gathered around her bed, a familiar scratching noise was heard above Esther's head. A message scrawled across the bare wall read, "Esther Cox, you are mine to kill!" There was no doubt in the minds of those present and especially in that of the doctor that the body of Esther Cox was possessed.

Whenever Esther left the home, the manifestations in the Teed residence would stop. When she went to live with neighbours, however, the poltergeist went with her.

In one such incident, Esther went to live and work on a farm and when the farmer's barn was destroyed by fire, Esther was charged with arson. She was convicted and sentenced to three months in jail. However, after wiser heads in the community prevailed, Esther served only a month.

When she returned to the Teed home, Esther may have been greeted warmly by her relatives, but not by the poltergeist. No sooner had she settled in, than fire balls, chairs, and utensils flew from wall to wall.

When the news of the Amherst poltergeist spread, people from all over the world converged on the town of Amherst hoping to witness such manifestations. One such man was an American actor and writer who was interested only in making a dollar. His name was Walter Hubbell. He became friends with Esther and the whole Teed family. Following extensive research, Hubbell concluded that Esther was not a madwoman, but the victim of a poltergeist. Hubbell eventually wrote *The Great Amherst Mystery*, a highly successful book on these strange manifestations.

Hubbell knew a good thing when he saw it. So he took Esther with him on tour of Maritime theatres. He was hoping that while Esther was seated on stage, the poltergeist would made its presence known. But that was not to be, and the audience in Pictou, Nova Scotia, shouted "Fake, fake!" Hubbell knew he was not welcome, and got out of town immediately. A similar situation greeted him in New Brunswick, so he wisely ended his little enterprise.

It is believed that an exorcism by a Mi'kmaq medicine man eventually drove the demons from Esther's body. Whether it did or not is debatable. In time, however, Esther Cox was free of her demons and, like her father before her, married and moved to the United States, where she lived until her death in 1912 at the age of fifty-two.

The Esther Cox story is a classic case of a person possessed, and is also one of our more famous Maritime Mysteries.

I'll Dance with the Devil

*H*ere's another hand-me-down in jig time:
One day while I was sipping coffee at a Tim Horton's, a woman asked if she could sit down and join me. She was interested in my *Maritime Mystery* series on ATV and wanted to discuss her favourite mystery tales. One of her favourites, she told me, never made it to

television. She asked if I would care to hear it. "Of course," I told her. This is her story.

There once was a popular dance hall in Sydney, Nova Scotia, where all the young people of the surrounding areas went on Saturday nights. One particular Saturday evening, a beautiful young girl went to the dance against her parents' wishes. While there, the young woman suddenly jumped up, and swirling around the floor, hollered, "Who will dance with me? I'll dance with anyone—even the Devil himself!"

A hush came over the place. The musicians stopped playing and all of the dancers moved away from the girl, except a stranger, who seemed to appear out of nowhere. He walked slowly to the middle of the dance floor where the girl was waiting. Smiling down at her, this very handsome and dark stranger said it would be a pleasure and honour to dance with her. He wrapped his strong arms around her waist, and began swaying back and forth to the music. The young girl closed her eyes and rested her head on the stranger's chest. The other dancers became spectators. No one else danced; it was as if they were incapable of moving—as if there was some power keeping them in a trance. They were transfixed by the way the young girl and the stranger danced. When the dance was nearly over, the girl looked down and fainted. In the confusion, the stranger disappeared. When the young woman regained consciousness, she told the crowd that when she had looked down at the feet of the stranger, she had seen a cloven foot!

When she finished telling the story, the lady paused and said, "Well, what do you think? Is it a good story?"

"Certainly is," I told her. And I went on to tell her that I came from Sydney and had heard that story many times when I was in my teens. The dance hall in question was located at a place known as Nelga Beach, on the outskirts of the city. I also told her I spent many a Saturday night in that very hall dancing the night away, but keeping one eye out for a tall, dark stranger who may be interested in dancing with my girlfriend.

The lady's story is similar to others that are documented in Helen Creighton's *Bluenose Ghosts*. One such story discusses how a young girl in New Brunswick paid dearly for wishing to dance with anyone including the devil: Satan left his hand print on her back. The young girl was so disturbed, she died of shock.

In Parrsboro, Nova Scotia, there was another young girl who also loved to dance and she too made the mistake of calling on the devil— who is never far away or out of ear shot. Apparently, this young woman's boyfriend decided not to take her to the local dance. This disturbed her so much that she exclaimed she would go to the dance with anyone, including the devil. Satan heard her. No sooner were the words out of the young woman's mouth, when a fancy carriage pulled up to her front door and out came a handsome young stranger. The young girl had the time of her life and danced every dance with the dashing young man. When the dance was over, the stranger wished the young lady goodnight, and left. It wasn't long after the girl retired for the night, when a loud noise was heard coming from her room. When her family went to investigate, they found her dead. On her forehead was the imprint of a horse's hoof—the devils' mark. The roof of the girl's bedroom was torn away. The devil had exacted his price, and came back to collect it—her soul. We did mention, didn't we, to be careful what you wish for?

The Ghost of Dean Llwyd

Late one night in 1933, the Dean of All Saints Cathedral in Halifax rushed from the parsonage on an errand of mercy. Concerned only with reaching the bedside of a dying parishioner, Dean

John Plummer Llwyd raced across Tower Road and was struck down by an automobile. Death claimed the good Dean two weeks later.

Following his untimely death, members of the congregation noticed the Dean wasn't where he was supposed to be—in his grave! He was seen, or his ghost was seen, in the church!

Dean Austin Monroe, now retired, was not fortunate enough to encounter the ghost of Dean Llwyd, but he has certainly heard stories of members of the congregation who claimed to have seen him. Dean Monroe tells of one such occasion during Sunday evening service, when a member of the congregation recognized the ghost of Dean Llwyd moving about the church. The young woman claimed to have seen the spirit going into the pulpit and gazing out at the congregation. Then, with folded arms, he came down from the pulpit and disappeared behind the vestry door. When the service was over and everyone had left the church, the young woman, concerned and frightened, told the priest who was still on the altar what she had seen. The young clergyman assured her she wasn't seeing things. He too had seen the ghost of Dean Llwyd on more than one occasion. Sometime later, the church organist reported that while playing the organ during a Sunday evening service, he almost fell of his bench when the ghost of Dean Llwyd passed in front of him on the way to the vestry.

From all eye witness accounts, the spirit of Dean Llwyd appears only during Sunday evening service.

If that is so, perhaps while attending an evening service at All Saints Cathedral, you to may not only be filled with the holy spirit, but be witness to another kind of spirit. You will know when Dean Llwyd is near; you'll feel a cold rush of air as he passes by on his way up the aisle.

A Dollar Ghost

*W*e must go back more than a hundred years for this haunting. It involved a man by the name of Dollar who made a lot of money by operating a grist mill in the community of Emyvale, Prince Edward Island. There was just one problem: Dollar was the only Protestant in Emyvale, and since he made his living off the predominantly Roman Catholic community, he should, it was thought, covert to Catholicism. "No thank you," was Mr. Dollar's response to the proposal. Even his closest friend, Pat McCardle, pestered him to convert. In the end, Dollar gave in. He told his friend that he would never convert during his time on earth, but he allowed that he would probably die a Catholic! That was good enough for Pat McCardle and the good folk of Emyvale. But not for Dollar. The least sniffle, cough, or ache, and the community was ready to call in a priest. In time, old Dollar's days were numbered. His doctor advised everyone that Dollar had only a few hours to live. Pat McCardle hurried to the bedside of his old friend and whispered in his ear the promise he had made. Dollar remembered and agreed to the conversion. Pat wasted no time. He saddled and mounted the fastest horse in his stable and headed for Kinkora, some sixteen miles away, to fetch Father James Duffy. The men were less than a mile away from Dollar's home, when the priest pulled up his horse and told Pat to slow down, "He's gone," said Father Duffy, "it's too late." Did old Dollar know all along that he'd die a Protestant before the priest arrived? Some die-hard Catholics thought so.

When Dollar's estate was settled, the grist mill was bought by a Jim McCloskey and his brother-in-law. The new owners continued to operate the mill the same way old Dollar did: opened early in the morning and closed down at 6:00 P.M., or when the last customer's order was filled. But, something was wrong. Somehow, things were not quite the same. Late at night when no one was in the mill, the machinery would start up on its own. This appeared impossible, since the mill was powered by a water wheel that had to be opened to start it up and closed to shut it down. People began to whisper that the mill was haunted by none other than Dollar himself. There had been other unexplained and strange happenings since old Dollar's death. One instance involved the new owner's mother who went to the barn one evening to bring hay down from the loft. No matter how hard she tried, she could not push the hay through the loft hatch. It was as if someone was deliberately holding the hay back. When she told the workers what happened, they all agreed that Dollar was haunting the place.

Father James Duffy was called in to cast out the offending spirit. When the exorcism was completed, Dollar's spirit was trapped in a bottle. The elders of Emyvale agreed to bury the bottle across the river from the mill where a strange and large black dog, perhaps a Scottish deer hound, was later seen and heard howling at night. Somehow they felt there was a connection between the dog and Dollar.

Once Dollar's spirit was entombed in the bottle, it was blessed and buried. After that, the dog never again appeared and the machinery in the mill fell silent during the night.

In time, a normal way of life returned to the community and it appeared that Emyvale's only Protestant was finally resting peacefully…or maybe not?

Father Duffy's Wake

You remember Father James Duffy, the priest who performed the exorcism of Dollar's spirit? Well, there's an amazing story connected with the exhumation of the good priest's body. It's unbelievable, but according to many witnesses, it's the gospel truth. This wonderful tale came my way from Leo Brendan Campbell of North Wiltshire, Prince Edward Island.

Father Duffy was born in Ireland in 1802. Following his ordination into the priesthood, he was sent to St. Mary's Bay, Newfoundland, where he served his community for the next eighteen years. From St. Mary's, he spent eight years in Antigonish, Nova Scotia, before being transferred to Charlottetown, Prince Edward Island in 1858. In time, Father Duffy was given charge of St. Ann's, lot 65, Kelly's Cross, and Kinkora.

During the winter of 1859, Father Duffy became seriously ill and was moved to Charlottetown, where he died on December 1st, 1860. He was fifty-eight years old. His remains were laid to rest in front of the church in Kelly's Cross. There, the gentle and holy father rested for the next forty years.

In 1898, a new church was built on the site of the old one and it was necessary to exhume Father Duffy's body and bury it, as had been his wish, in the shadow along the pathway to the church, so those who passed by would remember him.

On Saturday, September 15th, 1900, an event took place that the people of Kelly's Cross and surrounding areas would remember for the rest of their days—the date of exhumation. This was no ordinary exhumation—this was a saintly priest; a friend to one and all. Because of his status, the event became of interest to the local newspaper editor, who sent a reporter to cover the story.

This is what appeared in the *Charlottetown Examiner*:

Sunday, September 16th, 1900 was a day long to be remembered by the parishioners of Kelly's Cross. From early morning, streams of carriages could be seen converging on St. Joseph's Church and the reason for this immense throng was a four-fold ceremony to be performed that day. On Saturday, the day before, the body of Father Duffy, was disinterred and placed in a beautiful new casket that was provided by Mr. P.D. Hagan, the local undertaker, and placed in the church where his body lay in front of the main altar until Sunday Morning.

At 10 o'clock Sunday morning, September 16th, a Pontifical high mass was celebrated by his Excellency Bishop J .C. MacDonald, along with several other members of the clergy.

After the reading of the Gospel, an eloquent sermon was delivered by a former pastor, Reverend Patrick Doyle, of Vernon River. In his usual and vigorous polished manner, he spoke of the dignity, the power, the high office of, and the respect due to a priest of the Roman Catholic Church, which has been exemplified in the life and work of this servant of God, whose remains have for forty years enjoyed the peace and quiet in the old cemetery.

I began this Maritime Mystery by telling you that there was a startling revelation when the grave of Father Duffy was opened: To the amazement of those present, the body was in a perfect state of preservation! From the pulpit, Father Doyle said of this revelation, "What a joyous re-awakening of the dead past in the breast of those, who with loving hands tenderly laid away, forty years ago the remains of their beloved "Old Father Duffy," to gaze once again on that face they knew so well, resurrected for the moment, as it were, in the closing days of the nineteenth century."

There are a number of people still living who were present when the casket was opened by Patrick Duffy Maplewood, a very respected member of the parish who volunteered to do so, and who also saw the body as it laid in state in the parish church, and who testified to the truth of the event. According to reports of the time, others listed as witnesses were, Joseph Kelly, Gordon Waddell, Joseph Carragher, John H. Trainor, Mrs. Minnie Hughes, and Mrs. Maria Kelly. All were living witnesses to this strange event. Each of them states in his or her own way, "He was as fresh as he was on the day of his burial, there was no sign of decay. They even put a new suit and socks on the good father."

Since the people of Kelly's Cross had always regarded Father Duffy as a living saint, it was only natural when his body was found to be "as fresh as the day of his burial," that devotion to him intensified. Prayers were said to him, requests made of him.

Some of the senior citizens who were school-aged when Father Duffy's body was first lain in the old cemetery would go to his grave to offer a prayer and make a request. Some would even apply a pebble or clay from his grave and place it over a sore spot, to make it well.

We must caution that these are only personal and private beliefs and devotions and in no way have any official approval.

Did Father Duffy, lying in a cold grave for all those years, know that his so-called long sleep would be temporary, and that his body would eventual be interred in a more peaceful place? Was there some higher power in force—a power that kept his body from decaying?

Chapter Seven

The Unexplained

The Fork in the Grave

Can fear kill you? Can you actually be scared to death? Well, that's what appeared to have happened to Peter MacIntyre of Tracadie. This Prince Edward Island tale begins in a general store and ends in a graveyard.

Imagine, if you will, a cold wind blowing in from the sea, washing against the windows of a general store. The oil lamps flicker and cast ghostly shadows off the wall. The local farmers, gathered around the pot-belly stove, pause in their conversation and listen to the howling wind out side. After discussing politics, crops, and the weather, the topic turns to the supernatural. Most of the men have already heard Ben Peter's account of a brilliant light he once saw in the old French burial ground at Scotch Fort. But that isn't going to prevent him from telling it again. According to Ben's description, the illumination he witnessed rolled like a cart wheel and lit up the whole cemetery.

"Poppycock," scoffs Peter MacIntyre, "sheer nonsense and pure superstition."

To prove his point, Peter, will this very night, go into the graveyard alone and walk out the other side laughing. The other men who are gathered around the stove wink and smile at each other. A challenge has been made by a braggart. They would call Peter's bluff. A pound of tobacco is wagered.

Peter accepts the challenge and the rules are set down. He will take with him a hay fork and go to the centre of the graveyard and drive the fork deep into a grave to prove he was there. In the morning, the other men will go into the cemetery at first light and if they find the hay fork, Peter wins the bet.

Next morning the men go to Peter MacIntyre's cabin, but find it empty. Somewhat concerned, they rush to the cemetery. To their horror, they find the body of Peter MacIntyre slumped over a grave. When they roll the body over, they discover a prong of the fork driven through the tail of Peter's long black coat and deep into the grave.

Was Peter MacIntyre a victim of his own boasting? Or was there some other power at work?

The Dungarvon Whooper

A banshee-like scream is heard in the woods of the Miramichi. It's the wailing of the Dungarvon Whooper.

A story should not to be kept on a shelf or in a drawer. It should be told. So let the journey to the Miramichi begin.

In the 1850s, along the Dugarvon River near Whooper Springs, there were several logging camps. The cook of one such camp, was a young Irish immigrant who came to the new world to make his fortune. While the lumberjacks were working in the woods, the boss and the cook were alone in camp. The only interest the boss had in the young Irishman was the thick money belt around his waist. One day, when the lumberjacks returned to camp in the evening, they noticed that the cook was missing and asked the boss where he was. Shrugging his shoulders, he said "I guess he quit." Not so: a search of the camp found the body of the young cook. There is a theory that the boss had clubbed the cook to death, stolen his money and hidden the body in the barn.

New Brunswick's Michael Whalen, poet of the Renous, provides his own version of what happened in his famous ballad of the Dungarvon Whooper:

When the crew returned that night,
What a sad scene met their sight—

There lay the young cook silent, cold and dead,
Death was in his curly hair,
In his young face pale and fair,
While his knapsack formed a pillow for his head.

From the belt around his waist
All his money was misplaced,
Which made the men suspect some serious wrong.
Was it murder cold and dread
That befell the fair young dead
Where the dark and deep Dungarvon rolls along?

Unable to move out of camp because of a snowstorm, the men were unable to take the body to the nearest settlement for burial, so they carried it into the woods and buried the cook in a make-shift grave. No prayers were said over this young Irish lad's body. He lay there under a cold ground, unblessed.

That night, ungodly screams coming out of the forest drove the men from their beds into the night:

Pale and ghastly was each face,
"We shall leave this fearful place
For this camp unto the demons does belong."

Hurriedly, the lumbermen fled the camp for good. The owners kept hiring new workers but when they heard the terrible screeching of whatever was in the woods, they too fled. The owners had no other choice but to call in a Roman Catholic priest who read the church's exorcism prayer and blessed the grave with the sign of the cross.

Till beside the grave did stand
God's good man with lifted hand
And prayed that this scene would not prolong—

That these fearful sounds should cease,
That this soul may rest in peace
Where the deep and dark Dungarvon sweeps along.

It is said the priest's prayer silenced the horrible shrill sounds forever.

And round the Whooper's spring
There is heard no evil thing
And round the Whooper's grave sweet silence dwells.

But not everyone agreed. Some say the Dungarvon Whooper still wails like a banshee.

Be that as it may, the story of the Dungarvon Whooper is still, after nearly 150 years, the story most told around a warm fireplace. It's so popular that even a train was named after it. Should the reader visit Chatham, New Brunswick, we may share a pint and talk about what really happened that day so long ago along the Dungarvon. Where? Where else but in a tavern in the old Chatham Railway Station. You can't miss it—it's called the Whooper.

Granny's Ghost

This hand-me-down came to me on a Saturday morning in the local supermarket. I call the man who told it to me the "banana man" because as he recounted this familiar story, he was picking over the best fruit. It's a ghostly tale of a spirit who almost beat the family back home from the cemetery.

When the driver of the automobile came over the hill, he saw an elderly woman standing just outside the graveyard. She raised a small, fragile hand indicating she wanted him to stop. Why he stopped he couldn't say. Ordinarily he would have kept on going. But something he couldn't explain or understand compelled him not to. The woman got in the back, and leaned her head against the seat. The driver couldn't help but notice how sickly she looked. Her skin had a distinct pallor to it. The dress she wore was black with a white collar and cuffs. "Where are you going," the driver asked.

"I'm going home." She gave the driver the address and fell silent again. Someone's grandmother, he thought. But what was she doing by herself in the cemetery? Oh well, it takes all kinds. When he turned to ask if he was going in the right direction, she was gone! The driver pulled over immediately and stopped the car. The only thing remaining in the back seat was a lingering lilac fragrance. The woman had simply vanished!

The bewildered man was about to turn the car around and continue his journey when he remembered the street address she had given him. He drove the car slowly down the street until he came to the house. He stood outside for a moment trying to decide what to do, before knocking. Would the people inside think him crazy? He knew he had to find out. His knock was answered by a young woman. The man could hear voices inside. He told her about the woman he had picked up outside the cemetery and that she had wanted to be dropped off at this address, but had suddenly disappeared, vanished from a moving car. He described the elderly woman and what she was wearing. The young woman began to weep. "The person you're describing is—was—my mother. We just buried her—only just returned from the cemetery."

The Ghost of Ashburn

*L*ocated on the outskirts of westend Halifax, Nova Scotia, is the famous Ashburn Golf and Country Club. For more than seventy-five years, Ashburn has been the home for thousands of golfers.

There is something else on the course besides would-be Tiger Woodses that sets Ashburn apart from any other golf course in the country: it has a resident ghost. She's been seen on several occasions over the years watching from the tree-line. We're told she's old, very old, and tall and thin. This female spirit has been haunting the course and the area since the 1850s. According to local folklore, the woman became difficult in her old age, and got lost in the woods on several occasions. The last time she disappeared, she was found hanging from a tree. There is another theory, though, on how she died and why she's haunting Ashburn. Seems there was this old man who lived in a shack in the same woods. He was found dead quite by accident in his bed by hunters. Official records show he died of natural causes. When authorities investigated further, however, they uncovered a shallow grave and found the remains of an old woman. No one really knows what the relationship between the old man and woman was. Some believe they were brother and sister. Authorities at the time assumed, because her body was found near his shack, that he had murdered her.

The new members of Ashburn are not aware of the ghost; those who are try to keep an eye on the ball and not the woods. We've been told there are some golfers who, if they slice a drive into the woods, refuse to go anywhere near the tree-line in fear of coming face-to-face with the ghost of Ashburn.

We understand there have been moments in the clubhouse following a pleasant round of golf, when the conversation turns to why those easy putts were missed. Some put forth the theory that it's as if an invisible hand were involved. Older members look at each other and smile.

Too Many Coffins

*T*t was midnight when the brothers of the local Masonic order left the lodge. Little did they know what was ahead of them. There is but one explanation for what happened—they were in the wrong place at the wrong time. They were simply spectators of the restless dead. The frightful tale happened over a hundred years ago, just outside Sheet Harbour, Nova Scotia.

The lodge members lived on the other side of the harbour and to get to their boats, they had to cross a desolate stretch of road. There was a full moon to guide their way and the breeze coming off the water was a welcome relief from the suffocating smoke-filled rooms of the lodge. As they stepped onto the road, a sudden noise startled and confused the group. They stood there huddled together, listening. It was difficult to believe but the terrible sounds were coming from somewhere beneath them. The sounds were like no others they'd ever heard. It was a horrible mixture of wailing, weeping, and agonizing screams. And then the road beneath them began to shake violently and lift under their feet. Before their very eyes, the road was suddenly filled with decaying coffins that gave off a sickening odour. These containers of death moved in a zig-zag fashion, forcing the men to side-step in fear of bumping into them. From that indescribable nightmare, they watched as mystical shapes oozed through the walls of the coffins. These phantoms crept close to the ground, circling the men's legs and, like a finely spun web, wrapped themselves around the bodies of the paralyzed intruders. The brothers were now beyond fear. They were in an hypnotic state following the shapeless mass of nothingness that fluttered before their eyes. They would later recall that these phantoms took on a human quality, but then the shapeless faces would fall away into a vapor-like mass.

Suddenly, it was over—ended as abruptly as it had begun. It was as if the coffins and the ghosts were swallowed up by the earth.

The brothers fled to their boats. As they rowed in silence to the other side of the river, the sounds of tormented souls could be heard coming from that other world.

Those who were caught up in that ghostly nightmare are gone. So is the Masonic lodge. The only reminder of that night of terror is the road. Today, locals refer to it as the old ghost road.

A Frog's Frog

*I*f you have a sense of history when you first arrive in Fredericton, New Brunswick, and, the building that will immediately attract your attention is the officers quarters that was built in 1839.

Today, the building houses a special museum that's operated by the York-Sudbury Historical Society. There is a Maritime Mystery of sorts here. Hermetically sealed in a glass case squats the world's biggest frog. This is no run-of-the pond frog mind you. This lily-pad dweller weighed in at forty-two pounds. Is it a froggy fraud you ask?

In pursuit of the truth one need only journey to the nearest fishing hole. You must learn not to rush these rod and reel weavers of truth and tall tales; patience is indeed a virtue. Between baiting fish hooks and long pauses you'll hear the story of how the world's biggest frog came to be.

"We must go back in time," the old man with the fishing pole says.

Not back to Jurassic time mind you, only to a hundred plus years and to Killarney Lake, which is located a few miles outside of Fredericton.

The main character in this tale is a Fredericton hotel operator and outdoors man by the name of Fred Coleman. One evening while fishing on Killarney Lake, Coleman noticed a tiny frog sitting on a lily pad, watching him. Coleman was so taken by the little fellow that they became fast friends, and Mr. Coleman began feeding his new friend a rich and varied diet of insects and, according to some, a lot of human food and drink—whiskey to be exact. It didn't take long before our little amphibian friend puffed up to forty-two pounds!

But nothing lasts forever; Coleman's friend made his final jump, rolled over, and died. Coleman was devastated, so he had the big fellow stuffed and put on display in his hotel lobby."

While most New Brunswickers accept the Coleman Frog as the real thing, there are skeptics who say he's a fake, that he was made by a nineteenth-century chemist who put him in his drugstore window to advertise his homemade cough medicine—frog in the throat remedy, I suppose.

Who would dare poke a finger in Mr. Frog's tummy to see if he was just so much hot air? I kept my hands in my pockets. Whether he's all stuffed up or just paper-maché, will probably remain a Maritime Mystery.

The Phantom Train

There have been many stories of sightings of phantom ships sailing off into the sunset, and of phantom coaches drawn by black horses disappearing into the night, but it's rare to hear of a phantom train. Prince Edward Island has one.

This incident supposedly happened over a hundred years ago in Wellington.

The community hall in Wellington was only, as the old timers say, a "spit and holler" from the railway station. Well, many years ago, a wedding reception was being held there, and around midnight, above the music and dancing, everyone was stopped in their dancing shoes by the mournful whistle of a passing train. "Strange," an elder said. "Very strange indeed," said another. Strange because there was no scheduled train running that late at night. "We should go outside and see," said another elder. When the wedding party went outside they were dumbfounded by what they saw. Pulling into the station was a mainline locomotive. What made it all the more unbelievable to these country folk were the ghost-like people they saw boarding the train.

Some even swear they heard the familiar "All aboard," as the train pulled out of Wellington station.

Others reported only hearing the ghost train, not actually seeing it. They heard the train's whistle, then the familiar sound of steam and steel rolling over the rails.

Could it have been a soul train coming to collect the recent dead?

The Clock

*T*his fascinating Irish gem is from one of Dorothy Dearborn's tales from the other side. It's the story of Irish spirits stealing aboard ships for a ghostly voyage to the new world, not instead staying under the old sod where they belong.

The Irish who came to the Maritimes brought with them not only their personal belongings, but also their folklore, superstitions, and perhaps even unspeakable things from the spirit world, such seemingly harmless items as clocks

Consider the clock the Flanagan family brought to Fredericton, New Brunswick, during the great Irish immigration to New Brunswick.

When I produced this story for my Maritime Mystery series, I spoke with Charles (Mousie) Flanagan, who told me that the story was gospel.

Here's how he tells it: My Grandfather's clock was just an old-fashioned mantle timepiece made of some kind of dark wood. What was peculiar about it is that no one could remember if the clock ever worked. But it did chime on rare occasions. My father remembers it striking in the middle of the night once. In the morning they found Uncle Tom in bed, dead.

About two weeks after Uncle Tom died, my mother died—that was in May 1928—and the same thing happened. The old clock that had never worked, or kept time, chimed again in the middle of the night. The next morning my mother was found dead in bed.

Sometime in June 1937, the clock struck once again, and this time I heard it. It was in the middle of the night and everyone was asleep. The clock had only ever struck twice before. The next morning, our housekeeper wasn't up when we came down to breakfast. When we went to check, we found her dead in her room.

Well, my father got very angry. He went into a rage. 'That son-of-a-bitch-of-a-clock will never strike for anyone again!' he said.

He grabbed the clock off the mantle and took it outside to the woodshed where he took an axe and smashed it to bits. Not satisfied with that, he burned the wood and trashed the metal workings beyond recognition. Then he sent what was left to the dump.

Charles Flanagan ended the story of his grandfather's clock with a great sigh.

As I drove away from the home of Charles Flanagan, I was reminded of stories about haunted things; of people finding discarded pieces of wood from haunted houses, of Grandma's old rocking chair, even Grandfather clocks. Tic, toc, what's inside the old clock?

The Curse

Here's another great Island tale. What do you do when a mysterious illness or an unexplained force takes your loved ones? Do you stay or flee?

This ghastly little horror story can be found in F.H. MacArthur's *Legends of Prince Edward Island*. The journey begins on a farm where a young man's life hangs in the balance.

Nearly two hundred years ago in the farming community of Cape Wolf, Prince Edward Island, a young farmer by the name of Ronald MacDonald was the unhappy sole survivor of his family. He realized that if he didn't want to suffer the same fate as his parents and sister, then it was time to flee—he could no longer cope with the demons, if that was what they were. He had just buried his mother and father, and a few months before, his only sister. Ronald walked away from the farm where he was born, raised, and worked the land with his father.

He stopped at his neighbour's home to tell him he was leaving for good. The old farmer nodded in agreement and told the young man that under the circumstances, he was making the right decision.

Young MacDonald agreed, but told his neighbour, that were it not for the family curse, he could be happy living and working on the farm. The curse was put on MacDonald's great grandfather, who had murdered a young girl back in Scotland. It was a curse that would not be lifted until the last member of the MacDonald family died.

The old farmer said he had attended the funerals of six members of the MacDonald family, who all died of some mysterious illness.

The young man told his neighbour that he hoped to start a new life in the United States. They shook hands and the farmer watched the young man disappear down the road.

The next morning, the body of young Ronald MacDonald was found lying along the side of the road. He had died without a struggle. Was his death caused by the old Scottish curse?

Τhe Bone Knockers

*M*ost ghost stories can be dismissed as just that—stories. But there are people who have a personal experiences they feel simply can't be explained away. One such incident happened over sixty years ago in East Noel—usually a tranquil rural community— on Nova Scotia's Cobequid Bay.

East Noel resident, Reta Laffin remembers that in 1938, around supper time, a sudden loud noise sent everyone racing outside to see what was happening. Reta was only ten at the time, but remembers the older folk in the village saying the noise sounded like human bones knocking together. The mysterious sound put the adults on edge, and kept the children indoors that night.

Over the years, Reta has wondered if there was a reason for the unusual noise. She recalled an old story about a cruel schoolmaster who, back in the 1860s, may have started it all. He went to his grave with more than just pallbearers in attendance. According to Reta, his coffin was swarming with frogs and insects all the way from his home to the cemetery. It was when he was buried that the noise began.

The bone-knocker story has taken its place in the folklore of the Maritimes, and people like Reta Laffin have also written about the incident. Should it happen again, there will be a record, and for the record, Reta Laffin does not scoff at such things. She's a true believer of things from the other side.

Chapter Eight

Forerunners and Forecasts

The Wynard Ghost

*I*t was a late winter afternoon in the year 1785 when two officers of the 33rd Regiment were pouring over maps in the barracks in Sydney, Nova Scotia. One was Lieutenant George Wynard, and the other was Captain John Sherbrooke. Sherbrooke would eventually serve with distinction under the command of the Duke of Wellington in the Peninsular War, and in time, would be appointed Governor in Chief of Canada.

On that fateful afternoon while the officers were studying maps, a movement in the room caught the attention of Sherbrooke. When he looked up, a tall young man appeared in the doorway. According to Sherbrooke, the stranger wore the mantle of death. When Lieutenant Wynard saw the man, he grabbed Sherbrooke's arm and gasped, "Great God in heaven, my brother!"

They watched as the young man retreated back into the bedroom. Wynard, still shaken from the experience, followed Sherbrooke into the room; the bedroom, however, was empty. What baffled the young officers was that there was no other way out of the room except through the map room.

As the days passed, young Wynard anxiously awaited news from home. He often spoke to fellow officers of his younger brother's ill-health. There was nothing he could do but wait and pray.

Finally, mail arrived from England. There was a letter, not for Lieutenant Wynard, but for Captain Sherbrooke. In the letter, the family asked that Sherbrooke inform their son that his younger brother John had passed away. It was later noted that young Wynard had died in England at the precise moment his ghost had appeared in the map room in Sydney.

The incident of the Wynard ghost was the topic of conversation throughout military circles. Even the Duke of Wellington, Sherbrooke's old commander in the Peninsular War, had some choice words to say about the ghost: Wellington reminded his officers that there was a lot of heavy drinking in Cape Breton at the time, and suggested that perhaps what Sherbrooke and Wynard had seen were spirits that came out of a bottle. Wellington may have dismissed the story out of hand, but officers who were present at the time of the incident did not. During an inquiry, they confirmed everything that Sherbrooke and Wynard witnessed.

It's been over two centuries since the Wynard ghost first appeared in that barrack map room in Sydney, Nova Scotia. The garrison is now part of history and the principal players are all but forgotten, but not the Wynard ghost. It is forever part of our Maritime history.

The Forerunner

We walk among them, these Maritimers who, for a brief moment in time, are the victims of a forerunner—a frightening glimpse into one's future; a witness to one's demise.

Hand in hand a young couple went out on a cold October afternoon for a leisurely stroll down a country road. They spoke of their future, of having children and of growing old together.

Suddenly, they saw something up ahead that sent a chill through the young man; he didn't know why, but it bothered him. He couldn't make out what it was because of the cloud of dust it was kicking up. Then, out of the dust, six black horses appeared, and sitting on a magnificent carriage were two men dressed in black. The young man drew his sweetheart closer to him and told her they should move to the shoulder of the road to allow the horses to pass. She turned her face to his and with a puzzled look asked, "Where? I don't see anything."

"You don't see the horses and carriage?" asked the young man.

"No, nothing," she said. The young man drew her still closer to him, then stepped back and waited for the horses to pass. When the horses were nearly abreast of them, he realized it was a funeral procession. Another cold chill went through his body when he saw the six pall-bearers, with their heads bowed, walking slowly behind the carriage—they were all relatives of his fiancée!

The young man wondered if he was witnessing a forerunner? He remembered as a child hearing old people talk about such things.

He took his fiancée in his arms and held her close. Over her shoulder he watched the funeral procession vanish and again wondered if it was her funeral that passed them by on that lonely country road.

The Bell Tolled Death

*I*t was the morning of October 7 in the year 1853 when the passenger vessel the *Fairy Queen*, with eight passengers and a full crew on board prepared to set sail from Charlottetown, Prince Edward Island, for Pictou, Nova Scotia. Four of the passengers were women from the Kirk of St. James. For some unexplained reason, the bell of the Kirk of St. James began tolling while the ship was getting ready to leave.

At about the same time a Captain Cross, a man of habit, was on his way to the stables to prepare, as was his custom, for a ride in Victoria Park. On his way he was surprised to hear a church bell ringing. The good captain was aware that the sounding of the bell at such an early hour could mean that a vessel was in distress, so he headed for the waterfront, but found nothing out of the ordinary. Still tied up at the wharf was the *Fairy Queen*. In the distance, he could hear the pealing of the bell. Captain Cross hurried uptown toward the sound of the bell—toward the Kirk of St. James. As he drew nearer, he distinctly heard the bell toll eight times. The captain was surprised to see, at such an ungodly hour, three women dressed in white robes standing in the doorway of the church. There was yet another woman. She was inside tolling the bell. Just as suddenly as they appeared, the mysterious women vanished inside the church. When the captain tried to open the door, it was locked.

Captain Cross was soon joined by the church minister and sexton. When they opened the door and went inside, they saw three women climbing the steps to the belfry. The bell tolled for the eighth and last time. When the three men searched the belfry they found it empty and the bell's rope securely tied. Where did the women go and who was ringing the bell, and why?

Just before noon, the *Fairy Queen* set sail for Pictou.

The next morning, news spread throughout Charlottetown that the *Fairy Queen* had failed to arrive at the Pictou, Nova Scotia, wharf.

The *Fairy Queen* had left Charlottetown under a strong wind and a heavy sea. Off Pictou Island, the vessel began taking on water. She eventually broke up and sank. Of the sixteen passengers, nine had survived.

An inquiry would later show that the captain and crew had deserted the vessel, taking the only lifeboats and leaving the passengers to a watery grave. In his own defense, the captain told the inquiry that he went into the lifeboat to direct the lowering of the passengers, but a crew member cut the rope, leaving the stranded passengers screaming to be taken off the doomed vessel.

The heavy seas were too much for the *Fairy Queen*; she capsized, sending the passenger into the turbulent waters. Nine of the sixteen passengers clung to a floating piece of wreckage and some eight hours later were rescued.

The next morning, a boat was sent out in search of the *Fairy Queen*. She was approximately four miles from Pictou Harbour. There was no trace of the four women who perished.

A plaque on the north wall of the church is to this day a reminder of the sinking of the *Fairy Queen* and to the memory of those four of its members who went down with the vessel.

Could it be that the women Captain Cross saw in the church doorway were actually ghosts of the women about to lose their lives? And that the tolling of the bell was a foreshadowing of what was yet to happen?

The spirits of the Deep

Coal was discovered on Cape Breton Island more than three hundred years ago. By 1870, more than twenty mines were operating and employing thousands of men including children as young as nine years old. At any moment life could be snuffed out in those black dungeons, and perhaps the spirit of more than one wanders the corridors of abandoned mines including 26 Colliery.

Coal mines are an alien and unnatural world, without sun, sky, or ocean. It's a place of flickering light and shadows where one's imagination runs wild. Deep in a coal mine, what causes one to hear doors slamming shut and heavy footsteps running over a cobblestone street? And where do those sorrowful sounding voices come from? Is it all in the mind?

Retired miner Miles Guthro recalls such moments while working in 26. On more than one occasion, he had the feeling something other than human was standing next to him. Neil Johnson, a retired underground manager, told of what he calls a forerunner experience.

While making his rounds one day, he heard a very distinctive moan. When he went to investigate, he could not find the source of the sound or anyone nearby. Suddenly, the heavy equipment started up on it own. When Neil climbed up on one of the machines to investigate, he lost his footing, and got caught in the machinery. When he looked down, he saw a shoe lying on the ground, then realized it was his. While recovering in hospital, there was an underground explosion in number 26. The explosion occurred in the exact spot where he had been injured during a shift he would have worked, in an area where he would have been. No one can convince Neil that it was not a forerunner that saved him from certain death. What Neil remembers the most about that incident is the moaning; he still hears it to this day.

Coal miners are a superstitious lot. Catch a woman taking a shortcut over a mine and the miners will drop their shovels, pick-up their lunchpails, and go home for the day.

The Witch of the Miramichi

*I*n the early 1800s, Stellarton, Nova Scotia, became a booming coal mining community and men from all over came to town seeking work.

Others came to town to take advantage of the new industry. These were the entrepreneurs: the shop keepers, restaurant owners, apothecaries, and undertakers. Among those business types who arrived to set up shop was a strange and mysterious woman who sold the future. She was a palmist, a fortune-teller, a reader of cards and tea leaves. Her predictions, however, went beyond the usual, "You'll meet a tall, dark and handsome young man who will share with you a life of romantic bliss."

There are no known photographs of the lady of mystery. According to local history, she came to Nova Scotia from New Brunswick, where she had been known as the Witch of the Miramichi. In Stellarton, she was known only as Mother Coo.

In 1873, her first prediction came true when a group of local coal miners' wives were out for an afternoon of fun and decided to visit the fortune-teller. She looked at the cards, read the tea leaves and became frightened and distraught at what she saw. Mother Coo told the women there would soon be an explosion in the Westville Mine, which was located only a few miles from Stellarton. On May 13th of that year, her prediction came true. Fifty-five miners lost their lives in the underground explosion at the Westville colliery. Mother Coo not only became famous throughout the area, but was also feared by many. Mothers warned their children to give her house a wide berth.

In 1880, Mother Coo looked up from a teacup and again predicted there would be a mine disaster—this time the Stellarton Foord Mine. When her latest prediction became known, a miner by the name of James Lennon gambled on working one more shift: Lennon had planned to book passage to Boston for himself and his family the following day. James Lennon never made it to Boston. He was one of the fifty casualties of the Foord explosion.

On the Sunday morning following the tragedy, a priest mounted the pulpit and prayed for the dead miners, and denounced Mother Coo branding her a witch! Her days in Stellarton were numbered.

One hundred miles west of Stellarton lies the mining town of Spring Hill. On a Saturday morning, February 21st, 1891, dawn clears bright, but cold, as six hundred miners prepared to go below. On the minds of the miners and their loved ones was the final prediction of mother Coo: just before Easter there will be a terrible explosion in the Springhill Mine. Her prophesy caused great concern in the community, and to relieve the minds of the people of Springhill, mining engineers double-checked every piece of a equipment, all support beams, and methane gas levels. They found nothing that would suggest an explosion was imminent. However, on that faithful morning, six hundred miners went below and 120 of them never came back.

What happened to Mother Coo, the witch of the Miramichi? No one knows. She simply vanished. Some say back to New Brunswick. Perhaps she read her own tea leaves and saw she had no future, and wisely disappeared.